Turned

Clare Revell

Turned

Contact Information: titleadmin@pelicanbookgroup.com

Cover Art by Nicola Martinez

White Rose Publishing, a division of Pelican Ventures, LLC
www.pelicanbookgroup.com   PO Box 1738 *Aztec, NM * 87410

White Rose Publishing Circle and Rosebud logo is a trademark of Pelican Ventures, LLC

Publishing History
First White Rose Edition, 2014
Print Edition ISBN 978-1-61116-368-1
Electronic Edition ISBN 978-1-61116-367-4
Published in the United States of America

Dedication

For Andy, the best brother any girl could ask for. Even though he lives thousands of miles away, he's never far from my thoughts.

Praise for Clare Revell

Monday's Child

The blend of romance and suspense is superb, and the depth of emotion is so very touching. I am eagerly looking forward to the rest of the books in this series. Clare Revell is truly a master novelist. What a treat! I highly recommend *Monday's Child* to anyone looking for a GREAT story. ~ Mary Manners

Tuesday's Child

Ms. Revell has a marvelous touch with heroes. I love it! She also knows how to keep you on the edge of your seat! This is certainly turning out to be a great series! I can't wait for the next one! ~ Donna B. Snow

Tuesday's Child

Clare Revell...puts the EEP in creepy! *Tuesday's Child* has it all—deaf heroine, cop hero, orphaned child, and terrifying killer. This book kept me reading late into the night (with the doors locked and the brightest light on!). ~ B. Norris (Amazon review)

"If My people, which are called by My name, shall humble themselves, and pray, and seek My face, and turn from their wicked ways; then will I hear from heaven, and will forgive their sin, and will heal their land." ~ 2 Chronicles 7:14

1

Horns blared in the hot, muggy, late September evening. Amy Childs drummed her fingers on the rim of the leather clad steering wheel. The staccato rhythm was almost at odds with the country music blaring full volume from the stereo. *One, two, three, four. One, two, three, four.* She gazed at the line of traffic in front of her. What was the hold up this time? Surely the council wasn't digging up the roads of Filely again? Didn't they have anything better to do?

One, two, three, four. One, two, three, four...

Having been delayed at work because the till didn't add up, she now had less than an hour to get home, shower, change and be across town for Rosalie's baby shower. She and Rosalie had been best friends since school. Amy'd had a couple of boyfriends, none of whom lasted beyond a month, whilst Rosalie had fallen hard and fast for Ray Malone, the assistant pastor of the church they'd attended while at university in Scotland. Rosalie and Ray had married just after Ray had amazingly accepted the call to become pastor of a small church in Filely, on the coast of North-Eastern England. Rosalie's baby was due in two weeks.

Not having any ties, Amy had moved down there with them. She found a small house on the sea front and a job working in a hardware store and loved it. Well, loved it most of the time. She did a bit of everything; ordering, stock taking, and the till... And it wasn't her fault the till was wrong either. The twenty had slipped down the back of the register. It was there all the time. She hated being accused of something she hadn't done.

One, two, three, four. One, two, three, four...

She dragged her thoughts back to the evening ahead, and glanced in the driving mirror. Her long blonde hair was a mess. Brushing her fingers through it, she found sawdust. Great. There was no way she could avoid washing it before going out tonight. She'd bought the most adorable outfit and made a blanket for the baby. She needed to wrap them and box up the cake she'd made. And write the card. The flowers were in the garage in a bucket of water. Hopefully they hadn't wilted in the heat.

Her fingers kept drumming. *One, two, three, four. One, two, three, four*. She sighed. "Oh, come on. This is ridiculous."

The car in front of her moved. "Blow this, I don't have time to sit here and wait." She checked the lane to her right and pulled out, doing a U-turn. She swung wide, her mind a million miles away. A car horn blared in the queue behind her. "You can just wait a minute, mister."

She kept going, pulling the wheel hard over, keeping the turning circle tight. Could she do it in one? A pedestrian appeared in front of her. There was a sickening thud, and she slammed on the brakes.

Her heart pounded, and she sat frozen in her seat. *I hit him...oh, God, forgive me, I hit him.* Her fingers whitened on the steering wheel. Nausea rose and she swallowed hard. Shaking started in her hands and spread throughout her entire body. She'd hit him.

Amy closed her eyes. She could still see his face, stamped indelibly on her memory. His wide, staring eyes, fear and tension in his body. His blue shirt and tie, jacket slung over his arm and briefcase in his hand meant businessman not manual worker. The way he'd been scooped up by her car, tossed onto her bonnet and windscreen, then back onto the road replayed over and over.

The windscreen was cracked. It'd cost a bomb to replace as the insurance wouldn't cover it. *You just hit a man...forget about the windshield.*

A crowd gathered in front of her car, but she didn't move. She just sat, shaking, trying not to cry or throw up.

Sirens echoed and blue lights flickered. She was going to be late. She needed to call Rosalie and let her know. One hand fumbled for her phone. She found Rosalie in the contacts and hit call.

Ray's calm voice answered. "Pastor Malone."

"It's Amy..." she whispered. "Ray...something happened."

"What's wrong? Are you OK?"

Someone tapped on the window. Amy gasped, jumped and twisted her head. A uniformed officer stood there. She hit the button on the door, opening the window.

"Would you step out of the car please, miss?"

She didn't move. This had turned into a nightmare she couldn't awaken from.

"Put the phone down and step out of the car." The officer's tone hardened.

Ray's voice echoed in her other ear. "Amy, who's that? What's going on?"

She dropped the phone. Her fingers fumbled first to unbuckle her seatbelt, then the catch, finally opening the door. She got out of the car. Her legs buckled, not wanting to hold her up. She glanced to her right. The guy in the blue shirt lay on the pavement, surrounded by police and paramedics. A huge crowd of onlookers stood everywhere. "Is...is he dead?"

"No. What's your name?"

"Amy."

"Amy what?"

"Amy Childs." She couldn't tear her eyes away from the scene.

"Have you had anything to drink in the last hour?"

"No. I don't drink."

"Breathe into this until I say stop."

She frowned. "I told you, I don't drink." But she did as the police officer asked. "Can I go now? I have somewhere I have to be."

"Amy Childs," the police officer spoke firmly, pulling her hands behind her back. "I'm arresting you on suspicion of dangerous driving."

"What? It was only a U-turn..."

"You do not have to say anything, but it may harm your defense if you do not mention, when questioned, something which you later rely on in court. Anything you do say may be given in evidence." Metal cuffs snapped around her wrists and firm hands put her into the back of the police car.

"But it was only a U-turn," she repeated.

"U-turns are illegal," the cop said sharply. "And you hit a pedestrian." The door slammed shut.

Amy looked at it. It had no handle on the inside. She swallowed hard against the rising nausea as the car started to move. What had she done? Tears burned her eyes.

The journey was short. The officers led her inside the custody suite to the desk. The place stank of sweat and sick. She gave her name and address and handed over all her belongings. The officer took her down to a cell and removed the cuffs. She had to take off her shoes and leave them in the corridor. The door slammed shut, leaving her alone.

Amy sank onto the hard bench and buried her face in her hands. One small mistake and she was being treated like a common criminal. She hadn't meant to hit him. It was an accident. It was only a U-turn.

❧❧

Detective Sergeant Dane Philips pushed the bowl of now soggy cornflakes back in front of six year old Vicky. "Eat it."

She shoved it back at him, the milk slopping over the edge of the bowl onto the table, shaking her head violently.

"You eat cornflakes every morning."

Vicky mimed shoving her fingers down her throat and throwing up.

Dane sucked in a deep breath, trying to contain his frustration and anger. "Eat it. There are starving children in Africa who'd be grateful for that."

She waved at the cereal and shoved the bowl hard enough to send it flying off the table and smashing onto the floor.

"Now look what you've done," he yelled. "Pick it up."

Vicky wrapped her arms tightly around her middle and scowled at him, shaking her head. She didn't even have to say "make me" for Dane to know that's exactly what she meant.

"I don't have time for this." Dane broke off as the doorbell rang. "Don't you dare move, young lady." He strode to the front door, flinging it open.

His partner, DS Nate Holmes stood there, shirt sleeves rolled up and his tie loose in his collar. "Ready?"

"No." Dane snapped. "Vicky is on hunger strike and Jodie won't get up. In fact, Vicky in her own unique way just told me to send her breakfast to the starving children in Africa because she doesn't want it."

"What you need is a nanny," Nate joked.

"Don't tempt me. Can you cover?"

"Afraid not. The Guv wants us both to attend the meeting this morning, remember?

Dane sighed. It had totally slipped his mind. "There is no way I'm going to make it. You'll have to go by yourself." He paused. "You managed as a single parent for years. You never told me it was this hard."

"It had only ever been me. Plus, Vianne is my niece, not my daughter. Let me handle Vicky while you get dressed and drag Jodie kicking and screaming out of bed. I'll send Adeline a text. We'll drop the girls at mine and she can take Vicky to school." Nate pulled out his phone, texting quickly.

"Thanks."

"Welcome." Nate slid his phone into his jacket

pocket and headed into the kitchen.

Jodie appeared at the top of the stairs. She was twelve going on fifteen. "Is that Uncle Nate?"

"Yes. Now get down here and eat before you make me later than I already am."

"No."

Nate pushed open the kitchen door. "Jodie Kathlyn Philips, get down here this instant."

Jodie scrambled past Dane and into the kitchen.

Dane closed his eyes. *Why do they act up for me and not for anyone else, Lord?* Jasmine had been dead two years and it was still as hard as it had been in the days and weeks after her murder. Maybe Nate was right and a nanny was the answer. He could have someone live in, and solve the problem of late nights and long hours. His parents and in-laws were great, but there were only so many times they could help out.

Silence had fallen in the kitchen. He peeked around the door. Nate stood with hands on hips, staring at both girls who were sitting and eating. Dane shook his head and using sign language told Nate he should give up policing and become a nanny.

Grateful the girls weren't watching as Nate shot a sarcastic reply back, he nodded and headed out to get ready for work. Sometimes the sign language they used to communicate with Nate's deaf wife was a blessing in disguise.

☙❧

Amy sat in the interview room, her head in her hands. She was tired. A night in the cells wasn't exactly conducive to a good night's sleep. She wanted a shower, a decent cup of tea, and this whole nightmare over. She'd refused her one phone call. She had no one to call. At least no one she wanted to know about this. As the duty solicitor coughed, she looked up. "Now what will happen?"

"They'll lay formal charges and take you to court for the hearing. If you plead guilty, they'll bail you until sentencing. Otherwise you'll be bailed until a court date is set."

"Why won't they do it now?"

"The judge will want records and reports and so on done first. And the crown will need time to prepare its case. That could be several months."

"Oh." She swallowed hard, feeling sick again. "How long will it be if I plead guilty?"

"It'll probably be a couple of weeks or so."

Amy pushed her hands through her hair. "I don't understand. People get run over all the time and nothing gets done. Why am I made out to be any different?"

"If the person simply walks out in front of the car and the driver wasn't doing anything wrong, then they can't charge him. The fact is, you broke the law by doing a U-turn. You weren't driving with due care and attention."

"I didn't mean to hit him. I just had someplace else I had to be. I was in a hurry." Her conscience hit her sharply. This mess was her own making. The man she hit was innocent and she hadn't so much as given him a second thought or asked how he was in all the long hours she'd been here. "How's the bloke I hit?"

"The hospital released him with just cuts, bruises and a minor concussion. He's going to be fine."

"Good." She looked down. She'd missed the party. How was she going to explain this to Rosalie and Ray?

He was her pastor. How did she tell him she'd broken the law? He'd condemn her for it. She'd prayed all night for forgiveness and for this to just go away, but it hadn't. Did that mean she wasn't forgiven?

The door opened. "This way." The officer's tone was curt, and she stood slowly. He led her back to the desk and stood beside her.

The custody sergeant's gaze was icy. "Amy Childs, you're being charged with careless driving. You will be taken to the magistrate's court for the plea hearing. Then brought back here."

Amy started trembling as they led her out to the van and shut her inside. She was still trembling when she stood before the magistrate, her voice almost failing her when she had to confirm her name and address. She listened to the charges and when asked how she pleaded, replied "Guilty."

Because she was. She'd broken the law and hit someone one. She could have killed him. The judge bailed her for two weeks until sentencing on the condition she hand her driving license in to the court officer.

"But I need it for work," she whispered. How was she meant to do the few deliveries now? Never mind get to work. That's if she didn't get the custodial sentence she was warned was a possibility. Then she'd lose her job, too.

The judge called the next case, and she followed the official out. She handed over her driver's license, and was led to the van. At the police station she signed the paperwork, and was given her bag and phone.

The screen was full of missed calls and texts from Rosalie.

The duty solicitor looked at her. "Can I give you a

lift anywhere?"

"No," she whispered.

"Can I call someone to pick you up?"

Tears burned her eyes. "No."

"OK. See you back here in two weeks. Don't be late."

"I won't." Amy headed out into the street, walking slowly, not really caring which way she went, so long as she ended up at home. She could still see the man's face as the car hit him. The way he tossed into the air and landed almost in her lap.

A car horn blared and she jumped back from the edge of the road. Her heart pounded in her ears as a black car sped by. She needed to pay attention or she'd end up run over as well. Somehow she made it home and let herself in. She shut the door, noticing a black car drive by slowly. She locked herself in and headed to the stairs. More than anything else right now, she wanted to shower. Not that she'd ever be clean again.

The phone rang. Tempted to ignore it, she didn't. "Hello."

"Amy its Rosalie, what happened to you last night? Are you OK? You were talking to Ray, and then got cut off. After that you just didn't answer your mobile at all." She barely paused for breath before asking again, "Are you OK?"

Amy sank down on the stairs. "No..." Tears fell unimpeded. "I did something...and now I'm in so much trouble..."

"Ray will come get you, hon. Just sit tight until he does."

Not even having the strength to argue, Amy sat there and sobbed.

The next two weeks she lived in a dream. She shut herself off from everyone, including work. She didn't eat, didn't sleep and didn't attend church, so convinced she was that everyone condemned her. She was still praying that God would provide a way out of this mess. Rosalie had moved in with her and, as glad as Amy was of the company, sometimes she longed to be alone.

The day of the sentencing arrived. She had no idea how to get to court other than walking. She hadn't asked Rosalie to go with her, and wasn't going to.

Rosalie came into the hall as Amy grabbed her jacket. "Where are you going?"

"Court. Have to leave now if I'm walking."

"You're not going alone. Ray and I will go with you this morning."

Her heart sank. "What if...what if they lock me away?"

"It won't come to that."

"But it might. I looked it up on line. It could be a maximum of five years."

"We want to be there. He'll come and pick us up in about twenty minutes."

"OK."

Rosalie hugged her. "Whatever the outcome, God will give you the strength to deal with it."

Amy shook her head. "I keep asking Him to make all this go away. I prayed for forgiveness and trust He's done that, but why is this still hanging over my head?"

"He *has* forgiven you, but you still have to deal with the consequences of your sin. That doesn't just vanish, no matter how much you want it too."

"Oh."

"Because it wouldn't be fair otherwise, would it?"

"Guess not." She sighed. "I feel sick. If...if the worst happens, sell this place. Put the money into an account for the baby. This letter gives you access to everything you'll need..."

"Amy..."

She pushed it into her friend's hand. "Please."

Rosalie sighed. "OK."

A little over an hour later, Amy stood before the court, her heart pounding and stomach turning. Her palms wet, it was all she could do not to throw up. She acknowledged her name and address again and stood there, terrified as the judge looked at her.

"Amy Childs, you have pleaded guilty to one count of careless driving. The court has taken into account your previous unblemished driving record. However, by performing an illegal U-turn, you then lost control of your vehicle and knocked over a pedestrian, namely Derek Saunders. You were lucky not to have killed or caused him serious injuries. It is the judgment of this court to hand down a twelve month custodial sentence..."

Amy gasped, the blood rushing to her feet. She clung tightly to the rail in front of her.

"...to be suspended for a further period of twelve months. Should you reoffend during the period of suspension, you will be immediately sent to jail. If you do not reoffend, the custodial sentence will be removed. You are also banned from driving for twelve months. You may step down."

Behind her in the public gallery someone muttered, "That's not justice."

Amy left the courtroom sandwiched between Ray

and Rosalie, still shaking. Someone bumped into them and a gravelly voice apologized. Amy glanced up into the face of a stranger. Tall, with short cropped black hair and a scar on his cheek. His gaze slowly slid down her figure and then he nodded and moved on through the lobby of the court house.

Rosalie hugged her. "It's over, hon," she said, handing her the letter. "Here, I don't need this anymore."

Amy hugged her back. Not wanting to believe it, because it still felt as if she were dreaming, she looked at her friends. "Is it really over? Can I go home now?"

Rosalie nodded, then pulled a face. "Actually, I think we should go to the hospital first. The baby's coming."

§§

Dane stood outside the newsagents and watched the ad being slotted into the window display. He took the burger Nate held out to him. "Thanks. What do you think?"

Nate read the card. "Surprised you're not using an agency. You need anyone you have looking after your kids qualified and checked out."

Dane rolled his eyes. "I'm not completely stupid." He sat on the wall and unwrapped the burger. He pulled out the gherkins and licked his fingers slowly. "It just feels like admitting I can't cope."

"It isn't. I had help with Vianne before I married Adeline. Jas wouldn't want you struggling. She'd be the first to tell you to get help in. And a nanny is the only choice right now. Unless you're going to put them into before and after school clubs."

"Just hope someone applies soon. Figured she can have the spare room. Light household chores, kids' rooms, and the kids' laundry and so on."

"And a Christian I hope?"

"Would be nice, but I'll settle for trustworthy."

❧❦

Amy got off the bus, hating the daily commute even more now. This was no way to travel and was costing her more than petrol did. To get to her job across town, she needed two buses each way. She'd already been warned once about time keeping. At this rate, she'd lose her job before she got her license back. Actually, she'd probably lose it before Christmas and with a criminal record, she'd be hard pressed to get a new one.

She paused outside the front of the bike shop. She'd passed this every day for months, but hadn't considered the idea. But now…she could go straight to work. No more bus fares. No hanging around for ages if she missed one, or waiting in the dark for a bus, or sitting on her own while that creepy guy sat opposite her and eyed her all the time.

She caught sight of a black car in the window and shook her head. She was seeing the same car everywhere. Rosalie told her she was being silly and she wasn't being followed at all. But Amy wasn't so sure. Things had been strange since the court case and she was convinced it wasn't just her guilty conscience. Although it could be. Filely was a small town and you always saw the same cars during rush hour.

She went into the store and didn't take long in deciding which bike to buy. She also got lights,

14

reflective jacket and a helmet. Having paid, she left the store and rode her new purchase the rest of the way home, wondering why she hadn't thought of this idea sooner. A black car passed her at least twice. Filely seemed to be infested with black cars. Still it made a change from silver autos.

Arriving home, Amy wheeled the bike into the house and parked it in the cloakroom. She picked up the mail and shut the front door. The answerphone flashed on the side, and she hit the message button.

"Hi, it's Rosalie. Just to say we'd love dinner tonight. See you around seven."

Beep.

Then there was silence followed by heavy breathing. Amy sighed. "I thought changing my number would have gotten rid of you." She hung her jacket up, grabbing the phone as it rang. "Hello."

Silence greeted her. Followed by the heavy breathing.

"Get lost, creep." She hung up. The phone rang again, instantly. "Look, this is bordering on harassment," she sighed. There was no point changing the number again. She'd even gone ex-directory, and that hadn't helped. Kneeling down, Amy unplugged the phone at the wall. "Take that."

She went into the lounge. A black car was parked opposite the house again. She shook her head. "I'm just spooked, that's all. The phone calls are getting to me. It's a perfectly innocent black car. And if the others are coming for dinner, I best get cooking." Finding a CD, she inserted it into the stereo. She always found Berlioz relaxing and turned the volume up as loud as it would go.

Amy pulled the table out and laid it for the three

of them. She looked at it to make sure she hadn't forgotten anything, and then headed into the kitchen to start dinner. Grabbing a glass from the cupboard, she opened the fridge. Orange or apple? Orange. She filled it and turned around to face the window which overlooked her small, but totally enclosed back garden.

A man stood in front of the kitchen window, looking in at her.

Amy screamed and dropped the glass. It smashed, orange juice and glass shards flying in all directions.

The doorbell rang. Her heart pounded as she backed into the hall, terrified the man would come through the back door. Had she locked it? She had no idea. Reaching the front door, she put a hand on the latch. "Who is it?" she managed, her voice more of a high pitched squeak than anything else.

"It's Ray and Rosalie." Ray's voice was calm, but did nothing to allay the panic filling her.

Amy flung open the door, giving into the tears burning in her eyes.

He took in the look on her face. "What's wrong?"

"There's someone in the garden..."

"Stay here." Ray strode towards the kitchen.

Rosalie shut the door and hugged Amy tightly. "It's all right."

"It's not all right. That car's been parked out the front for days. It's following me. Thought I was imagining things, but now..."

"There's no one there." Ray came back into the hallway. "Do you want me to call the police?"

Amy shook her head, her whole body trembling. "No. They won't do anything. And anyway, you said he's gone now."

"You should still call them."

Rosalie led her into the lounge, taking the baby in the car seat.

A car screeched to a halt outside and almost instantly, a brick smashed through the window. Both women screamed, and the baby began crying.

Ray reached for the phone. "Now I *am* calling them."

Amy sank onto the couch. "It won't work. I unplugged it because of the calls..." She ignored the look he gave her as he pulled out his mobile instead. *How did things get so screwed up? I didn't mean for all this to happen... The papers say Mr. Saunders is OK now and the courts have dealt with me. I know You've forgiven me, but I still feel awful.*

The police came and went, taking details and leaving her a crime number for the insurance company. Ray boarded up the window. "Come back to ours tonight."

"I can't..." Amy paused. "I never gave you dinner. I'm sorry."

"It's fine. We'll get take out instead. Once we get you safe and settled at our place."

"I'm not letting them push me out of my own house. I'll be fine." She saw them out, noticing the black car still opposite the house. She shuddered at the dead bird on the doorstep and made a mental note to clear it up in the morning.

Just after two in the morning, Amy jerked awake. Smoke drifted through the open bedroom window and an orange glow lit the garden. Jumping out of bed, she ran to the window and pulled back the curtains. The compost heap was alight and threatening to engulf the back fence. Not thinking, she ran downstairs and outside, grabbing the garden hose. She turned on the tap and aimed the jet of water at the fire.

Alternating between the compost heap and soaking the fence panels, it took her half an hour to put out the fire. She raked over the compost, making sure all the sparks were gone. Then she headed slowly inside. She wrinkled her nose. It still smelt smoky. Pushing open the door to the hallway, she found flames licking up the inside of the front door.

Fear pulsed through her again, and she ran for the water jug from the fridge. Tossing it on the flames, she listened to the crackle become a hiss and the light faded. She headed into the lounge and sank down to the floor. "I don't believe this. What more can possibly go wrong tonight? It can't be a coincidence. Two fires, a brick, the man in the garden. But why?"

Pulling over the laptop, she fired it up and then typed Derek Saunders into the search engine. She ignored the reports of the accident, which had her name plastered all over them. Instead she went for the smaller articles. The name Saunders itself flashed up several times. Kevin Saunders was the former leader of some gang or other before becoming mayor earlier in the year. The police could never pin anything on him — hence his town council role...and he had a younger brother called Derek.

Shock filled her. That explained everything. No wonder the police weren't that bothered last night. If this Kevin Saunders was after her, she was a marked woman. Tiredness swept over her and she lay on the couch, praying that God would show her a way out of the mess she'd gotten herself into.

The phone rang, waking her from a sound sleep. Ignoring it, she got up, and pushed her hands through her hair. A glance at her watch told her it was gone nine thirty, and she was late for work again. Shaking her head, she walked across the room and pulled the curtains, allowing the bright, warm sunlight to shine through the un-boarded part of the window.

Amy froze.

The same man, short dark hair, scar on his face, stood on the other side of the glass. He raised a cross bow and fired. The arrow smashed through the glass, straight at her.

2

Nothing changed, Dane sighed. He'd arrived home late the previous evening, to find his mother pulling her hair out over the behavior of the girls. Vicky had once again refused to eat and Jodie had come in, dumped her stuff on the floor and gone out. "Dressed to the nines" was the way Mum phrased it. No one had replied to the ad he'd placed. He was beginning to wonder if Nate was right and a nanny agency was the way to go.

And today already looked as if it would turn out the same way. He arrived at the nick, late again. He sank into the chair behind his desk as nonchalantly as he could. Nate slid coffee over to him and he picked it up and smiled at his partner. "Morning, Nate."

"More like afternoon. Which one was it this time?"

Dane checked his watch. "Not quite afternoon— it's barely nine forty-five. And it was Jodie. She's getting worse. What did I miss?"

Nate leaned back in his chair. "Not much—just a murder in Clarkdale Street." He tossed Dane his notebook. "Uniform got the call about half four this morning. I got there a little after seven. Hence my afternoon comment. You can catch up on the way to the morgue."

"Thanks."

Nate grinned, getting to his feet. "By the way, the Guv's on the war path."

"Joy."

Detective Inspector Vanessa Welsh flung open the office door. Silence fell across the ten desks arranged around the room. "Dane. My office. Now."

Dane looked up. "Nate and I were just going—"

"Nate's a big boy. I'm sure he can find the morgue without you holding his hand. Just like he found Clarkdale Street without you earlier." She jerked her head to the door. "Don't make me repeat myself."

Nate dropped a hand on Dane's shoulder. "It's been nice knowing you, mate."

Dane sighed, pushing upright. "We who are about to die, salute you." He followed his commanding officer down the corridor to her office.

"Shut the door." Her curt tone only confirmed how much trouble he was in.

He complied and stood in front of her desk. "I know I was late and I'm sorry, Guv. If you let me explain…"

"I would really love to hear your explanation. You have been late consistently over the past few months. Late coming in. Leaving early. Long lunches. It's gotten worse recently. Sit down."

Dane perched on the edge of the seat. He laced his fingers together, the contents of his stomach curdling within him. The pounding in his chest increased.

"Well?"

"Kid problems."

"Really?"

He took a deep breath. "Neither of them will get up. Vicky won't eat. I spend a good hour each morning fighting with them."

DI Welsh looked unimpressed. "So do thousands of parents up and down the country. Why are they at work on time and you're not?"

"I'm doing it alone."

"You're not the only single parent in this station. Or in the country."

Dane took a deep breath. His reasoning sounded pitiful now. But it wasn't. His struggle was very real and he didn't know what to do.

"We all cut you some slack when Jasmine died. It wasn't easy losing her like that, especially when you were working the case."

He nodded slowly. The Herbalist killings were his toughest case to date and had made the national headlines when the Prime Minister and the investigating officer's wife were two of his victims. The only good thing to have come out of it was Adeline and her subsequent marriage to Nate.

DI Welsh continued. "But that was two years ago. You can't keep blaming your current problems on your wife not being here."

Dane narrowed his eyes, his hackles rising. He straightened, bristling. "So it's my failure as a parent, is that what you're saying?"

"I'm not saying anything of the kind. Just suggesting you prioritize things."

"So it's my kids or my job?" Anger flared through him, and he fought to contain it.

"Will you stop putting words into my mouth? Reorganize your child care arrangements."

"I've advertised for a nanny. Just haven't found one yet."

"Then until you do, perhaps your child minder could start a little earlier. Or you pull your kids out of bed at seven thirty and put them in the school's breakfast clubs. Or see if a neighbor could take them.

Who picks them up?"

"Either my parents or Jas's." He pushed his hands through his hair.

"Then sort it. You've got a week. Nate can't keep covering for you. It's not fair on him." She paused. "And if I've noticed, so have the rest of the squad and the rest of the chain of command. You're not just letting yourself down here."

"I'll sort it."

"Good. Now go catch Nate up at the morgue. Assuming he's even left his desk yet."

Dane exited the office, very much feeling like his tail was between his legs and his ears were down. Bile rose in his throat, and his tie choked him. He had no idea how to fix any of this. He loved his kids, and he loved his job. *Lord, I need some help here. A nanny would be ideal. Please provide someone of Your choosing.*

He looked at Nate. "You still here?"

Nate stood as Dane came over. "Figured I'd wait and this way we only use one pool car. Give the boss one less thing to gripe about. Let's go."

Dane grabbed his jacket. "Thanks."

"Are you all right?"

"Fine."

"Pull the other one, it's got bells on."

Dane shrugged. "Is my head still on my shoulders?"

Nate grinned. "There's a chunk missing, but you won't need that today. How bad was it?"

"Other than me letting down the entire squad, not to mention being the worst partner you could possibly have, and it's all down to being a lousy father who can't juggle work and kids effectively like every other single parent can? Things are just peachy."

"She said all that?"

"I condensed it for you, but essentially, yeah, that's what she said." He held the main door open, letting a blast of heat into the air-conditioned building. "I could read between the lines and go as far as saying I turn up on time from now on or I'm looking for a new job. She did say I can't blame Jasmine's death for the kids acting this way. It's been two years. Time to move on. And so, therefore, if it's not Jasmine's fault, its mine."

Nate held his gaze. "Why don't you just count your blessings for a change?"

Count his blessings? What blessings? Pent-up frustration boiled to the surface as his left hook caught Nate square on the jaw, sending him flying to the tarmac. "One," Dane snarled.

Nate lay there, slowly moving his jaw and rubbing it. "Feel better?"

Dane shrugged. He held out a hand to haul his partner to his feet. "I am really sorry."

"It's OK." He nudged Dane toward the passenger side of the car. "And at least you didn't do that upstairs."

"Then the Guv would have my guts for garters."

Nate looked at him over the top of the car. "Just forget it happened. Kids go through stages of hating their parents and testing the boundaries. That's what yours are doing right now."

Dane climbed in and slammed the door. "I've tried everything. But Jodie won't get up. She answers back. I get told 'if mum were here things would be different. She'd never speak to me like that.' How do you do it?"

"Honestly, now it's a lot easier as Adeline leaves after I do. But I'd just tell Vianne that if she's late then

I'm late and we're both going to get into trouble."

Dane fisted his hands. "I miss Jas so much. I can't do this without her."

Nate looked at him as he started the car. "What would Jas do with them?"

Dane thought quickly. "She'd pull the covers off them and threaten to send them to school in pyjamas."

"Then do it. And if that doesn't work, pray someone responds to your advert."

Dane nodded as Nate drove. "I'll do that."

"Good. It's time to take back control. Those kids need you whole again. And so do I."

Dane looked at him. "Huh?"

"You're barely functioning, mate. Even now. It's not what Jas would have wanted."

He nodded slowly, forcing his mind back to work and where they were going. "So this murder?"

Nate took a deep breath. "Like I said, the call came in first thing this morning…"

☙❧

Amy's breath came in small shallow gasps. Her heart thudded against her chest wall and pounded in her ears. She didn't dare move as the man stared in through the window at her. Then he turned and moved away.

The arrow still vibrated in the wall, a fraction of an inch from her head. Tears filled her eyes and spilled over.

She slid down the wall to the ground, shaking hard. A note floated to the floor beside her. It must have come in with the arrow. Trembling fingers opened it. *Justice will be served. Vengeance is mine. An eye for an eye, a tooth for a tooth and a life for a life.*

She closed her eyes, panic mixing with the fear inside her. *I have to go, Lord. Leave here. There is nothing else I can do. I can't stay. I thought this was over.*

Pounding came from the scorched front door. She jumped and gasped, clamping a hand over her mouth in terror.

"You can't hide in there forever, Amy Childs. You hurt my brother. You're mine. The courts let you off, I won't do the same. Watch your every step because I'm coming for you."

Footsteps moved away and after a couple of minutes, the black car drove off. She couldn't ask the police for help. She was a convicted criminal, in the same category as a murderer or the guy hunting her down. If she stayed here, she'd die. He'd already tried once with the fire and again with the arrow.

She ignored the small voice telling her if Saunders wanted to kill her, she'd be dead already. There was no way out but to run. She threw a change of clothes into a rucksack and pulled out the tin from under the bed. She checked to make sure the contents were there, before sliding it into the pack, along with several other things she needed. She ran her fingers through her hair. *I can't cut it. What about dyeing it?*

Dying... What if she were dead? There'd been a TV program years ago, where a man had pretended to drown in the sea and in reality gone off to start a new life somewhere else. She could do that.

She nodded at her reflection. She'd always fancied going red—even gone as far as buying the hair dye a while ago before losing her nerve, so that's what she'd do.

An hour later, she looked in the mirror at her red

hair. It was going to take some getting used to. She tied it back and shoved the towels she'd used into her rucksack. Pulling a hat over her head to hide her hair, she wheeled the bike outside and locked up the house. A pang of regret filled her at the thought of leaving everything behind. But she didn't have a choice.

The ride to the beach only took five minutes. Having locked the bike up on the prom, she headed down to her usual spot, which as always, despite the warmth of the day, was empty. She laid out her towel and put her book, sunglasses, and suntan lotion on it. She set her clothes in a pile next to it and ran her fingers over the phone for a long time before typing a message to Rosalie. *I'm sorry. Forgive me.*

Amy took a deep breath and hit send. This was it. There was no going back. Picking up only the rucksack, she stood. Her purse, along with all her cards, ID, and everything else that tied her to this life, she left behind.

Ducking under the pier, she started walking towards the station and the first train to London she could catch. From there she'd just pick somewhere and trust God to guide her some place safe.

❧

A day later, Amy got off the train in Headley Cross, some four hundred miles from Filely, just after ten thirty in the morning. She'd arrived in London far too late to do anything other than sleep on a bench the previous evening. Even the cheapest motel had wanted ID and a credit card for payment, and she didn't have either. Cash she had aplenty.

Headley Cross had been the seventh stop on the

seventh train out of London when she'd woken. She had no idea where she was, but trusted God had a reason for bringing her safely here. Now she needed to find a job and somewhere to live. Not necessarily in that order either, but preferably at least a room before it got dark tonight.

She could find a hotel, but that would only be temporary and again they'd want ID and a credit card no doubt.

And a church. She needed to find one of those, too.

Walking down the High Street, she paused outside the newsagents and read the cards in the window. Room to let...how much a month? She sucked in a deep breath. That was more than the rent on her entire house back home.

She ran her finger down the glass. Cleaner, gardener, nanny... The ad for the nanny expired today.

Live-in nanny required for immediate start. Two children age twelve and six. Light household duties, some cooking, cleaning, and laundry. £300 pcm. Ring D. Philips on 07595 648092.

The job had probably gone, but there was no harm in asking. A live-in nanny position would kill the two proverbial birds with the one stone. Amy pulled out her new pay-as-you-go mobile and dialed the number on the card. She paced as she waited for an answer.

"Philips." The curt male voice caught her by surprise. For some reason she'd expected a woman to answer.

"Hi. Could I speak to a D. Philips please?"

"Speaking."

"My name's Amy Stabler. I'm calling about your ad for the nanny in the shop window. Has the position been filled yet? The card expires today and—"

"No, the position is still open."

She sucked in a deep breath. "I'd like to apply for it."

"Wonderful. I can meet you over coffee to talk about it. Bring your CV with you. There's a café on the High Street, the Three-Sixteen. I'll be there in ten minutes."

Amy looked around, not seeing it immediately. "OK. See you then." She hung up and then realized she had no idea what the bloke looked like.

At least finding the café shouldn't be hard. She hoped.

Then she paused. She didn't have a CV and no time to make one up. She'd just have to be as honest as she could and hope and pray it would be enough.

❦

Dane hung up and looked back at Nate. "What's that withering glance for?"

Nate's eyebrow went higher. "You're meeting a snout in the Three-Sixteen?"

Dane shook his head. The Three-Sixteen was a Christian café run by the church both he and Nate attended, Headley Baptist. "No. That was someone asking about the nanny job. I'm going to interview her on my break. The ad runs out today so if she's no good I need to come up with another plan."

"Like an agency that checks out all their staff. Want me to sit in?"

"And freak her out?" Dane loosened his tie. "No. You can sit at another table and hide behind a paper. Let's go."

"You said ten minutes."

"I want to be early. Besides it's just over the road."

Three minutes later, Dane sat at a table in the corner, a mug of gingerbread coffee in his hand, watching people coming in and out. *Lord, if this is Your will, let her be the one. She's the only person who's enquired, and I'm running out of time.*

Finally someone he didn't recognize came in. She was stunning and young. At a rough guess he'd say mid- to late twenties. Her long red hair hung in waves to half-way down her chest. Her clothes were creased, yet smart. Nevertheless, she looked weighted down.

Brown eyes darted around the room. Was she looking for him or someone else? Was that her? She walked to the counter and spoke to Lia, the barista.

Lia nodded and handed her the drink that he'd already paid for.

The woman picked it up and walked to his table. "Mr. Philips?"

He stood up and held out a hand. "You must be Miss Stabler."

"Amy, yes." Her hand was cold and soft in his, but her grip was firmer than he anticipated. "Thank you for the coffee."

He indicated the chair opposite. "You're welcome. I could hardly invite you for an interview over coffee and make you buy your own. Have a seat."

"Thank you. I couldn't find my CV, I'm sorry. Is that going to be a problem?" She slid into the seat opposite him, setting her pack on the floor by her feet.

At the next table, Nate sat sipping coffee from behind his paper, but Dane knew he was watching them intently. And listening. And what's more, he could feel Nate's disapproval from here.

He shook his head and turned his attention back to

the woman in front of him, as he picked up his coffee. "Normally I'd have your CV in front of me, or at least read it in advance, but as I don't, how about we start with you telling me about yourself? Name, age, marital status and so on."

She sipped her coffee. "My name's Amy Stabler. I'm twenty-seven and single. I have GCSE's in English, maths, drama and theater arts, music, RE, French, history, and literature. All a grade C or above. As well as BTEC's in science and sport science. I have A levels in English, child development, and drama. I like singing, dancing, cross stitching, and I go to the gym two or three times a week."

Dane nodded. That was a pretty impressive list. But it left a vast amount of time unspoken for as she'd have left school ten years ago.

"Did you go to university?"

She inclined her head slightly. "I read English and Latin at St. Andrews in Scotland for my major and minored in drama."

He studied her as he sipped his coffee. Her pupils were fixed and her nostrils flared a little. Nate would insist she was lying, but he wasn't so sure. It could just be nerves. "Have you worked with children before?"

"I helped out in the crèche at the church I used to go to before I moved here. I also did a couple of years as a TA in a school."

"What's your current job?"

"Currently between jobs. The last one was in a hardware store, doing a bit of everything. I've also done cleaning."

That's a vast come down from working in a school. I wonder why. "OK. Well, I have two girls, ages six and twelve. I'm a single parent and work long, irregular hours, hence the need for someone to live in. You'll get your own bedroom, use of the lounge and so on. I'll expect you to clean the girls' rooms, do their laundry, lunches and cook for them the nights I'm not home in time. Also to do morning and afternoon school runs. You'll have sole charge when I'm not there. Obviously with the half-term holiday coming up, you'll need to entertain them."

"I can do that."

"How?"

Amy looked at her coffee. "Trips to the park, swimming, craft activities and so on."

He nodded. "Good answer. Whilst they're at school, aside from the light duties mentioned, your time is your own."

"OK." She nodded and hesitated slightly, opening her mouth and then closing it again.

"Go on."

"In the evenings...am I expected to keep to my room?"

"Not at all—unless you want to. I don't bite or watch football all the time. Feel free to watch the TV or read or whatever."

"OK."

He watched her, his copper's instinct on alert. "Is there anything else you want to ask me?"

She shook her head, finishing her coffee.

"Not even how much I'm offering to pay?"

"It mentioned it in the advert." She swallowed nervously, her hands tightening on the cup. "My last job was four-hundred-and-fifty a month, so it's a fair bit less, but then there's no rent."

Dane nodded. "I'm giving you board, lodging, and all meals. When I'm around you'll be off duty. So that's pretty much every evening, unless I'm working nights, and almost all weekends."

"OK." A faint smile crossed her lips. She was pretty when she smiled. She should do it more often.

He didn't often make a snap decision like this, but something, or Someone, was pushing him into it. "If you'd like the job, it's yours. When can you start?"

"Today if you want." She paused. "What about references?"

"We'll start with a two week trial." He tilted his head at the shudder that ran through her at the word trial. "If it doesn't work out, or you don't like it, then I pay you the two weeks and we go our separate ways. Do you drive?"

She looked down, her cheeks going a pale red. "No."

"OK, it's not a problem. The school is within walking distance, anyway. And the buses are pretty good. I'll meet you at the house at two. That will give me time to show you around, before we do the school run." He wrote down the address and gave it to her. "I'll need your phone number."

"Oh...right." She pulled her phone from her pocket. "I'm not sure how to find the number. It's a new phone...I lost the other one."

"Unless..." He pulled out his phone and checked the received calls. "Your number's still stored from when you called me earlier, I think." He hit redial and Amy's phone rang. He added her to his contact list. "There you go."

She picked up her bag. "I'll see you at two, Mr. Philips." She stood and headed to the door.

Dane sat down again as she left.

Nate slid into the seat Amy had just vacated and

put the folded newspaper on the table. "Well, she's pretty. How did it go?"

"She starts this afternoon."

"Really? On the basis of a fifteen minute conversation? You hardly know her. Did you get references, qualifications, experience?"

"She told me enough to hire her on a two week trail, which either of us can terminate if need be."

Nate rolled his eyes. "Dane, these are your kids we're talking about. She might have a record."

"No one else applied. The Guv is on the war path and as good as told me to sort something out or my job is on the line. What am I meant to do?"

"Use an agency." He shook his head. "And the fact she's young and pretty has nothing to do with it?"

This time Dane rolled his eyes. "You're a married man."

His partner pointed at him. "Married, not blind."

"Whatever, but it's a moot point. I'm old enough to be her father...well almost."

"That makes her what? Fifteen?"

"Twenty-seven."

"And you're forty-three. That isn't that big an age gap."

Dane rolled his eyes again. "Enough of the matchmaking. I need a nanny and she needs a job. And from the way she accepted so fast, ignoring a huge pay cut, somewhere to live as well."

Nate laughed. "Uh huh."

"I'll give you uh huh."

His partner tilted his head. "So I guess I'm covering for you *again* this afternoon."

"Just from two. So I can show her the house, school run, get her settled, meet the kids and so on."

"Fine, but it's the last time. We'll both be out of the office, working hard on this murder. Speaking of which, I had a text from the morgue. Professor Jacobs requests the pleasure of our company ASAP."

Dane rose. "Oh, that sounds like fun."

"Sure you don't want to be a stay-at-home dad?" Nate quipped.

"Shut up and give me the car keys. It's my turn to drive."

3

Amy walked down the street in shock. Had it really been that easy? No more than fifteen minutes, and she had a job *and* somewhere to live. Despite the drop in salary, she'd still be better off each month than she was before as she didn't have to pay the bills or buy food. And how hard could it be to look after two kids and a house? Even with half term coming up at the end of the month, it couldn't be that difficult. There must be plenty of things around here that they could do.

She'd been honest about her qualifications at any rate and the experience. It was enough she'd lied about her name without anything else. She stopped outside a clothing store, her mind whirling. She couldn't turn up without any clothes as that would just be too suspicious—and now she had a job, she could use some of her inheritance/savings. Going inside, she bought a week's worth of everything she'd need, including some thick sweaters, and a dress to wear to church on Sunday. Stuff that would be easy to clean and practical—but what amounted to a whole new wardrobe. Next she went into a chemist and bought bath and shower stuff, including toothbrush and toothpaste.

This really was turning out to be a new start. New clothes, new name…new her?

Actually, a suitcase would be an idea, she realized. After all, no one moved in to a new place without one, and turning up with bags of new clothes was going to raise a red flag if nothing else did. She had to blend in, act normal. Finding a luggage shop, she picked out a case similar to the one she had at home—Filely, she corrected. This town was home now.

She was dead. Had to stay dead, too.

To the amusement of the assistant, she packed all the shopping bags into the case. She picked up matching hand luggage and paid cash as she had everywhere else. At least she had plenty of that. Admittedly, most of it was in fifties, but she had about five hundred in tens and twenties in her new purse. The rest was in a tin in the rucksack. She just needed to find a safe place to keep it.

What else did she need? Other than a new handbag? A map for one thing. And ID. But she had no idea how to go about that. For now a library card would do. Something you didn't need proof of address for. She went back into the chemist and applied for a store card, filling in Mr. Philips' address on the form. Then she went to the library and did the same thing. At least now she'd have something with her new name on.

The one flaw in her plan was not having a bank account. Or a means of using her existing one without tipping anyone off. She couldn't open a new one without ID. She'd just have to ask to be paid in cash and say she'd sort out her own tax. Hopefully Mr. Philips would be all right with that.

Her thoughts turned to her dark haired employer. He seemed like a nice bloke. Older than she imagined, based on how he sounded on the phone, but not grey.

And very good-looking—swoon-worthy in fact. If she had to guess, she'd say late thirties, early forties. Certainly no more than forty-five. So even if he weren't her boss, he'd be too old to date. The only time the nanny married her boss was in novels. Certainly not in real life.

In any event, she reasoned as she headed to buy the last few bits she needed, she was on the run. Not looking for love or romance. A bus went past and an idea occurred to her. There must be a travel shop somewhere. She could get a bus pass with a photo ID. She'd look into it tomorrow. Along with researching fake IDs on the internet.

Amy glanced at her watch, then looked at the map. Arundel Road wasn't that far from where she was, if she was reading the map correctly, and she didn't want to be late.

There was just one more thing she needed to buy. A Bible. And reading notes. She found just the store she needed on the corner of the precinct. She wished she could have brought her Bible from home. Her parents had given it to her for her eighteenth birthday, but it would have been too obvious had it been missing from beside her bed, as it wouldn't have been left on the beach with everything else. The same as with her laptop.

Putting her new Bible in her hand luggage, she set off, following the map. She found the house fairly easily. There were two cars parked outside. Was she late?

Mr. Philips came out with another man. He had short dark hair as well, but was a totally different build, and was also decidedly cute.

"I'll see you tomorrow, Dane. Don't be late."

"I won't. Tell you what, pick me up about eight, and I definitely won't be." He grinned. "We'll shock the Guv by being early." He broke off. "Hello, Amy."

"Hi." She pulled the case up the driveway.

"Amy, this is Nate Holmes, a colleague from work and a friend from church."

She held out a hand. "Amy Stabler. Nice to meet you."

"And you." He shook her hand. "You must be the new nanny."

She nodded.

He grinned. "Good luck with that." He winked at Mr. Philips and did some strange hand gestures. "See you in the morning."

"Sure." He returned the hand gestures then turned to Amy. "Come on in. Let me take your case."

"Thank you." She followed him inside and took a deep breath as he shut the door. "What were the signs?"

He grinned. "Nate's wife is deaf. So we all speak sign language, even though she reads lips really well."

They stood in a large spacious hallway, with doors opening off each side. A flight of stairs curved around the center of the hallway. The house looked homely and tidy. Had he just run around with the vacuum cleaner, the way her mother used to whenever she knew visitors were coming?

"I'll show you to your room and give you the guided tour." He lifted her case and bag again and carried them up the stairs.

Amy followed him, running her finger along the edge of the bannister. Not a trace of dust.

At the top of the stairs, he turned left and headed to the end of the landing. He opened a door to a large pale yellow double room. "This is your room. It looks out over the front of the house, and has built-in wardrobes, en suite shower and loo."

Amy looked around in delight. It had a bay window. She'd always wanted a bedroom with a bay window. "It's lovely, Mr. Philips."

"Please, call me Dane." His eyes twinkled at her enthusiasm. He set her case by the chest of drawers. "I'll show you the rest of the house. The girls' rooms are just along here." He headed back into the hall and opened the door next to hers. "This is Jodie's room. And as always it's a pigsty." Pop group posters littered the maroon walls and there wasn't a scrap of carpet to be seen. The bed hadn't been made either. "Her choice of color, even if it is a little dark for my liking."

But this room won't be a mess for long if I have anything to say about it. "My room used to be like that when I was her age. I had a path from the door to the bed. I don't think I used a wardrobe or chest of drawers at all, until I found a huge spider in my clothes. After that I put them away and kept it tidy."

"That would work here, too." He shut the door and opened the next one. "And this is Vicky's room."

It belonged to a much younger child. There were dolls and teddies everywhere. It was pink and airy and again with an unmade bed. That would also change. Her father had drummed into her time and again the necessity of a made bed. And with a quilt, there really was no excuse not to straighten it each morning.

Dane shut the door. It seemed strange thinking of him by his first name, but that's what he wanted, so she'd oblige. "Here we have the bathroom, in case you want a bath instead of a shower, airing cupboard, and my room is at the other end of the landing."

He headed back downstairs. Amy followed, in awe at the size of the house. The lounge ran from front to back, with patio doors leading into a conservatory. There was a separate dining room with a beautiful table and matching chairs and sideboard. "We rarely eat in here," he commented wryly. "Unless we entertain and that isn't very often."

They went back into the hall. "There's the study and downstairs loo, and the door to the garage. The burglar alarm is here. It's really easy to set." He showed her. "The code is seventeen zero one."

She grinned. "I shan't forget that in a hurry."

Dane grinned back. "Yeah, it's done after the *Enterprise*."

"And why not? Nice easy number to remember, and a lot safer than using the first four digits of the phone number."

"My feelings exactly." He walked through into the kitchen—a huge spacious room with a breakfast bar and stools around it. Beautiful multi-colored tiles, black marble worktop and white cupboards lined almost every wall. Children's photos and paintings hung off the fridge with magnets. There was a spoon collection proudly displayed on the wall. A utility room opened off it with the back door leading outside. "Hoover, washing machine, tumble drier, and ironing stuff lives in here. When I start dinner, I'll show you the oven and so on. It can be a little temperamental at times."

Wow, just how big is this place? And he only wants me to clean the girls stuff? Does he have a cleaner, too?

"It's a lovely house. It must take a while to keep clean."

He slid his hands into his pockets. "More time

than I have some days, but I like to take care of it. Jas, my wife, couldn't stand things dusty."

She wondered what had happened to his wife. That was the first time he'd mentioned her. "Mum was the same."

He glanced at the clock. "We should go and pick up Vicky. Jodie walks herself home, but is usually in around three thirty, by the time she's finished gossiping with her mates and dawdling." He set the burglar alarm and headed out. "I need to introduce you to Vicky's teacher. They only let the children go if they know who's collecting them, if it isn't a parent."

"That's a good idea."

"Yes. The whole system was tightened after one of the kids was taken without authorization."

"Really? I didn't think that was possible."

"Nor did we. We found the child unharmed, but it could have been a whole lot worse. There was a pretty big police hunt for her."

"I bet. It's good she was unhurt." Amy paused. "You said *we* found. Did you help look for her?"

Dane nodded. "A lot of us did. It could have been any of our kids."

Amy walked with him, taking note of which way he went. "If you don't mind me asking, what happened to your wife?"

"She was killed almost two years ago." His eyes clouded, and his whole body stiffened.

"I'm sorry. What happened?"

"She was murdered."

Amy caught her breath. She hadn't expected that.

He stood still for a moment, his eyes glistening before he blinked and cleared them. "It's been hard on all of us. Vicky in particular. My parents have helped out a lot, but they're not getting any younger, and the girls can be a handful at times."

"Hence hiring me."

He nodded. "Yes. I'll work up a contract tonight, and we can both sign it."

"OK." She looked at the trees by the school. The autumn colors glowed in the sunlight. It was so beautiful. She didn't intend to waste a single moment of her new freedom.

"Hello, Dane."

Dane turned and held out a hand. "Hey, Pastor Jack. How are you?"

"I'm good." The bloke had auburn hair, the most amazing grey-green eyes and a captivating smile. No dog collar, so not Anglican and not in robes so not Catholic. There seemed to be no end of good-looking blokes in this town.

"How's Cassie?"

"Complaining she looks like a beached whale and hasn't seen her feet in weeks."

Dane nodded in agreement. "I remember that well. She hasn't long to go now, has she?"

Pastor Jack shook his head. "No, four weeks, give or take a few days. She's due November tenth. And I don't mind admitting the whole idea scares me to death."

"It'll be different this time, you'll see." Dane turned to Amy. "This is Pastor Jack Chambers, one of the pastors of my church. Pastor, this is Amy Stabler, my new nanny."

Amy shook his hand. "Hi. What denomination of church do you pastor? I'm looking for one to attend."

"Evangelical. You'd be most welcome at the services."

"Thank you. I'll do that."

"Then I'll see you Sunday." Pastor Jack headed in through the gate.

She watched him go, amazed at how friendly everyone was here. Or was it simply that everyone she'd met so far was a Christian?

She may have uprooted herself, but God had seen fit to plant her in the midst of His people.

❧❧

Dane held open the gate for her, then followed her inside. "I was going to ask you to come to church with us, just hadn't gotten that far yet."

She glanced at him. "We've had other things to talk about aside from denominations of churches. But it was on my list of things to ask you at some point."

He nodded. "Yes." The doors opened, and he watched for Vicky as the children spilled onto the playground. He had kept back the fact he was a cop. Something told him that he shouldn't tell her just yet, and he'd make sure the girls and Nate didn't let it slip either. He wasn't sure why, but knew this feeling came from the Lord, and therefore wasn't his to reason why.

Am I putting my girls at risk by hiring her, Lord? Maybe it's simply that she needs my help as much as I need hers and You want me to gain her trust first.

Vicky came running over and wrapped her arms around him tightly as if she hadn't seen him for years.

He swung her into a bear hug, the usual ripple of joy spreading warmth through him. "Hello, Vicks. How was your day?"

She shoved her painting—a man and a dog—right into his face.

"It's very good." He ruffled her hair and set her down gently. "Vicky, I'd like you to meet Amy."

She looked up shyly, pulling back into her shell.

He hunkered next to her, holding her hand securely. "Remember how I told you I was looking for someone to come live with us and take care of you and Jodie when Daddy has to work? Jodie called her a fairy godmother, rather than a nanny."

Amy grinned.

"Well, Amy is that person."

Amy knelt next to him and held out a hand. "Hi, Vicky. It's a pleasure to meet you. And I love the idea of being a fairy godmother. So long as I get pink sparkly wings."

Vicky nodded.

"Can I see your painting?"

Dane watched as Vicky slowly held it out. He didn't believe what he was seeing. His youngest daughter barely responded to anyone she didn't know. Just getting her into school had taken a major effort and even now a change of teacher or routine could knock her back.

"Wow. That's really good. Is that your daddy with the spiky hair?" Amy pointed and as Vicky nodded, gestured to the dog. "And who's this?"

Vicky shrugged, looking at her father.

Dane gave a grin. "I'm guessing its Auntie Adeline's dog, Ben."

Vicky nodded.

"I wish I could paint dogs as well as you. He's a lovely color, black and brown and white. He must be a King Charles spaniel."

Vicky nodded again.

"Ben is Adeline's hearing dog," Dane said.

Amy smiled, her whole face lighting up. "That makes him a very special dog."

Vicky seemed to be bonding with Amy. Relief surged through him. That was a huge weight off his mind.

Miss Macnin, Vicky's teacher, began walking toward him and he met her halfway. "How was she today?"

"She refused to do PE. Clammed up for an hour afterwards, hence the painting. There's a letter in her bag about the class homework. It fits in with the topic this half term. Mr. Philips, there was another matter. I was talking to a friend of mine, she's a child psychologist."

Dane's hackles rose, and he stiffened.

"I didn't mention any names or Vicky in person. Just said we had a child in the school that was having a hard time, but loved art and painting. She suggested maybe using the painting to get her to talk about what happened to her mum."

"She was only four when my wife was killed."

"But it's surprising how much she'll remember. Either way, it'll help her to work through what's bothering her. It might get her talking a little as well. This would help her integration with the other children immensely."

Dane nodded. At times the teacher sounded like a broken record over the talking issue. It wasn't as if Vicky was mute. She'd just decided not to talk. "I want to introduce you to Amy, the new nanny. She'll be dropping Vicky off and picking her up, if it's not me doing it now."

Amy waved from where she stood with Vicky. "Hi."

Dane looked at his daughter. They'd suggested counseling for her before, but he didn't see the need. She was a child and children bounce back. Vianne, Nate's niece, had been the same age when her parents died and she'd turned out just fine. Maybe he should encourage Vicky to use sign language, by signing to her each time he spoke.

Vicky walked up and tugged on his sleeve.

"What is it, honey?"

She pointed to the gate.

"Sure, we can go home. We need to show Amy what happens after school." He took firm hold of Vicky's hand, and glanced at Amy. "Milk and cookies, her favorite thing and guaranteed to put a smile on her face."

Amy laughed as they walked. "Now that sounds like fun. Have you ever tried dunking the cookies in the milk?"

Vicky looked at her with wide eyes and shook her head.

"You should. It's almost as good as chocolate."

Dane shook his head. "Then homework. Then an hour of TV before dinner if the homework is done."

Vicky scrunched her nose up and shook her head, pointing at one of the other boys from her class.

"Does he get all his homework done?"

She shook her head.

"Then he'll get in trouble. Miss Macnin said you have some tonight?"

She nodded slowly, rolling her eyes. She may not speak, but she had no trouble making her feelings known.

"OK. I'll have a look when we get home."

Vicky held his hand tightly as they walked the

short distance to the house.

Jodie sat on the doorstep, blazer undone, and hair disheveled. Her tie was peanuted and her shirt untucked, covered in something he couldn't identify. She leapt to her feet. "Where have you been? You're late. Again. And where's Grandma? She's meant to be taking me over to Rebecca's."

"Grandma isn't coming tonight. I'm here instead."

"So how do I get to Rebecca's house now? Because you won't take me. You never do."

Dane scowled. He'd suspected Jodie had his parents wrapped around her little finger and this just confirmed it. "Walk, maybe—use the legs God gave you for once? And I wasn't here because I had to speak to Vicky's teacher."

"Great. What's the freak done now?"

"That is no way to speak of your sister. I had to introduce Amy, otherwise she can't do the school runs."

"And who's she?"

Dane sighed internally, curbing his frustration. "This is Amy. She's the new nanny. She'll be living in the spare room and when I'm not here, what she says goes."

"Oh, really?"

He unlocked the front door. Jodie shoved past him and straight up the stairs, slamming her bedroom door. "That was Jodie."

Amy rolled her eyes in mock amusement. "Twelve going on nineteen."

He nodded grimly as he deactivated the burglar alarm. "If you'll excuse me, I need to go have a word. Vicky, can you show Amy where the milk, cookies, and glasses are?"

She nodded and headed to the kitchen, Amy close behind.

Dane took a deep breath and walked up the stairs for the inevitable fight with his oldest daughter.

ॐॐ

Amy looked at Vicky. She really didn't say anything and now that her dad wasn't there, she seemed to have shrunk several inches. Something had really traumatized the little girl and it was a fair guess it was the death of her mother. "So which cupboard are the glasses in?"

Vicky pointed.

Amy nodded and got down two. "Though I don't suppose Jodie will want one, will she?"

Vicky shook her head.

Amy put one back. "Will Daddy want coffee or milk?"

Vicky pointed to the kettle.

"OK, then we'll do him coffee."

Amy poured a glass of milk for Vicky and beamed as she reached down the box of cookies. "Oh yummy, homemade ones. They always taste heaps better. Did Daddy make them?"

Again Vicky shook her head. Oh, this was hard, but she wasn't going to give up.

"Grandma?"

This time she got a small nod.

Yelling echoed from above them. A door slammed, opened and slammed again.

"I think Jodie's in trouble," Amy said.

Vicky nodded.

Dane's voice increased in volume. "Jodie, don't

you dare walk away from me! Get back here now!"

"No!" Footsteps hurtled down the stairs, and the front door opened and slammed shut.

Amy looked at Vicky. If anything, she'd shrunk even further. "What about you? You get into trouble?"

She shrugged and made a wobbly hand gesture.

Amy leaned forwards conspiratorially and put a hand to the side of her mouth. "I get in trouble sometimes. Everyone does. It doesn't mean people don't love us though."

Vicky dunked the cookie into the milk. Her eyes were fixed on the door, but her tilted head showed she was still listening.

"I was wondering what we could do tomorrow after school. Do you like going to the park?"

Vicky nodded slightly.

Amy filled the kettle and put it on to boil. "Cool, because I love parks. We could feed the ducks. Maybe find the swing and slides. Would you like that?"

There was a slight nod.

"Brilliant, because I love going on the swings."

Vicky glanced at her and then waved her hands, making a tall and wide gesture.

Amy read between the lines and winked. "No one's ever too big to go on the swings. We'll go tomorrow."

Dane came in as the kettle boiled, his face set and his eyes glittering. "You read my mind." His voice was as taut as his shoulders.

"Tea or coffee?"

"Coffee, please, with just a little milk." He leaned against the counter, folding his arms tightly against his chest. "So, you got this letter about your homework then, Vicky?"

Amy made the coffee as Vicky pulled it from her bag and handed it to him. Amy added the milk and looked for sugar. She couldn't find any. She glanced over at Dane who was frowning over the letter. "Is there any sugar?"

He shook his head. "No, we don't have any. Vicky, I can't work this out. I'll look at it again later."

Amy watched as Vicky's face fell. She held out a hand. "May I?"

Dane handed it to her. "Be my guest."

She read the letter through twice. It could have been phrased in a much easier way, but she got the gist of it. "So you need to make a boat. We'll need something that floats then." She looked at her. "Does your glass float?"

Vicky pointed to the milk in it.

Amy clicked her fingers. "Good point. Why didn't I think of that? Try this one." She handed her an empty one.

Vicky put water in the sink and dropped the glass into it. She shook her head.

"Then we try something else. How about we check the recycling box?"

Vicky looked at her father.

"Go on. It's in the garden. I'm right here, not going anywhere."

Vicky slowly headed to the back door.

Dane looked at Amy. "Go with her. So long as she knows where I am, she'll be fine."

Amy followed Vicky into the large, well-cared for garden. Plants lined the borders, and a neat lawn filled the gaps between. She glanced at her employer through the kitchen window, wondering where he found the time to keep tabs on this as well as the house. He stood slumped against the counter, hands hung loosely by his side and his eyes downcast.

Vicky tugged on her hand. She held up a box, milk carton, washing up liquid bottle, a tin, and some wood.

She gave Vicky a thumbs up. "Let's go and try them out. Then we can design a boat. Take them inside to Daddy."

She followed Vicky inside. There must be a way to reach her. She just wished she knew what it was.

⊷⊷

Dane trudged into the lounge and flopped onto the couch exhausted. At least Vicky was asleep now and Jodie was in bed. Well, upstairs in her room, would be more accurate. The beginnings of a boat sat on the coffee table. He nodded to Amy who sat curled up and shoeless on the end of the sofa. "Thank you for helping her with that."

"It was fun." Amy smiled. "She's a cute kid."

"She seems to like you. She rarely responds to anyone she doesn't know."

"Does she speak at all?"

Sorrow filled him, and he shook his head. "No. After Jas's death, she just stopped speaking. She hasn't said a word or uttered a sound since. Sometimes Jodie will speak for her, but that depends on her frame of mind."

"I wonder why."

Dane stiffened. "Don't suggest child psychologists. She doesn't need one—she manages to communicate fine without speaking. Besides she wouldn't respond anyway."

"I wasn't going to. She'll probably respond

eventually, given time and love."

"Hope so." He pulled his laptop over. "This bounces off the router attached to the main PC in my room. I'll make you an account on here so you can use it."

"Thank you."

"Welcome. I need to come up with a contract. That's assuming Jodie hasn't put you off working here." He looked at her over the top of his reading glasses. "She can be a right little madam at times."

That was putting it mildly. She'd been downright rude and stand-off-ish. She'd even accused him of replacing Jas. A fact he'd vehemently denied, but Jodie didn't listen. He'd sent her to bed immediately after dinner, and she wasn't allowed to watch her favorite TV soap all week. He had no idea what was wrong with her. She'd been moody for the past few months, but this was a new low even for her.

Amy shook her head. "No. At her age, everything is a drama. She's bordering between wanting to be a child and being a grownup."

"She's twelve, nothing more than a little girl." His defenses went up automatically. He'd defend his kids to his dying breath and woe betides any kid or boy or man who laid a finger on them. Ever.

"She'll always be your little girl. Dad saw me as that, right up until he died. But all you have to do is look at her to see she's growing up."

Dane sighed. "I'm not ready for her to grow up."

"There isn't a lot you can do to stop it. Not even locking her in a tower like Rapunzel would fix that one."

"I can try." He typed as he chatted, trying to word the contract. At the same time he found himself loving the company. It had been so long now since he'd been able to talk about anything other than work. And talking about the girls this way was a relief. "I've tried to get through to her, but nothing. Maybe she'll respond to you."

"Maybe. But there are things that a girl never tells her father, no matter how much she loves him."

Dane looked up sharply. "She's twelve."

"And probably has a new boyfriend every week. I know I did at that age." She paused, studying her nails. "Just so long as she doesn't see me as a threat."

He straightened. Surely, she hadn't overheard the conversation he'd had with Jodie. "What do you mean?"

"I moved in. She probably sees me as taking her mum's place." She paused, tilting her head a little. "I overheard some of what she said. Well actually, it was difficult not to. But that is how any child would see it."

"You're her nanny. Not her stepmother."

"Probably just as well, as all stepmothers have horns and a pitchfork, don't they?"

Dane rolled his eyes. "As do I, right now."

Amy looked at him critically, her gaze running slow enough over his body to cause a burst of heat to flood him. He shifted in his chair. Finally her gaze returned to his face.

She tilted her head. "Can't see any, but then you're not yelling at me. Not so far, anyway." She winked. "Jodie simply doesn't see the distinction between the two yet. What do you usually do about food shopping?"

"Usually I do it at the weekends with the kids in tow."

"I can do it, if you want. I'll have time while

they're at school."

"You don't drive."

"One of the supermarket's in the precinct delivers free if you spend over twenty five quid—we had one like that back home which I used a lot. I can shop on the way home from school first thing." There was a long pause, and she looked down at her hands again. "If you want, it was just a thought. I don't want to overstep my place."

Dane peered at her over his glasses. Why the sudden change in her? She hadn't held back while talking about the kids, but suddenly her whole demeanor altered. "That would be good, thank you. I'll leave you some housekeeping. Also that way if the girls need anything, you can just go ahead and buy it."

Amy nodded. "I'm also happy to take them clothes shopping."

Relief filled him. "That would be wonderful. Although, that's another potential minefield where Jodie's concerned."

She tucked her hair back behind her ears. "I'm a pretty good negotiator."

Dane turned back to the laptop, working on the contract, while Amy flicked through the TV channels with the remote. He was struggling to phrase this and debated searching on line for ideas. Then he decided to just put in writing what they'd spoken about. Half an hour later he had something he was happy with and printed it off. "Here you go."

Amy took it and read it carefully. Then she signed it and handed it back. "It's fine."

"I figured a week's notice either way seemed fair for now."

"Yeah." She yawned. "Think I'll turn in. It's been a

long day. What time do they need to be up?"

"I'll wake them before I leave, but I need to be gone by eight. Again that varies each day. Jodie needs to be in school by eight twenty-five for the first bell, and Vicky by eight forty-five."

"No problem. Good night."

"Night." Dane let out a deep breath as she shut the door behind her. He reached for the TV remote. He'd catch the second half of the Rangers game before going up to bed himself.

It was so strange having a woman in the house again. He shoved to one side the insistent voice telling him he was betraying Jas. He wasn't.

Nate was right. Amy *was* very pretty, but she was his daughters' nanny not their governess. And he was definitely no Mr. Rochester.

4

Amy woke with a jump, convinced there was someone leaning over the bed. Her heart thudded against her chest wall, wanting to leap free of the constraints holding it. The door must be open, for a shaft of light shone in from the landing, slicing across the darkness of the room. It had been closed. There was no way she'd sleep with it open, not in a strange house at any rate. Reaching out, she flicked on the bedside lamp, bathing the room in a soft pink light.

She turned over and gasped. There *was* someone there. She wasn't paranoid after all.

Vicky stood beside the bed, her dark hair stuck to her head, her long white nightie emphasizing the paleness of her skin.

"Vicky, are you all right?"

Of course she wouldn't get an answer, but this time the child didn't even acknowledge her or move her head in response. Instead, her eyes stared at Amy; a hollow gaze that looked right through her. It was most unnerving to say the least.

"Vicky?"

Amy threw back the covers and sat. The only obvious explanation was that the child was sleepwalking. "Let's get you back to bed. It's chilly tonight." She stood and put a gentle hand on Vicky's shoulder, leading her, via the bathroom, back to her room.

Vicky got into bed, and Amy tucked her in. The child continued to stare for a moment longer, then closed her eyes and relaxed into the pillow.

Amy stood there for a few moments, to make sure Vicky was OK. Did Dane know about the sleepwalking? What really bothered the little girl? Maybe the teacher was onto something with the drawing. Could this be why she'd been led here to the seventh stop on the seventh train, to a town she'd never heard of? To help.

She returned to her room and closed the door. Getting back into bed, she turned out the light. Of course, she had enough of her own demons to fight and keep her from a decent night's sleep. She didn't want to close her eyes, afraid she'd see the accident again. It was amazing how a very simple, but very wrong choice could mess up your life and turn it in a totally different direction. Despite the fact she was running from someone who wanted her dead, perhaps for now at least, she was safe.

Until Dane found out the truth and fired her.

A pang of regret flooded her. How had Rosalie and Ray taken the news of her "death"? The tides around Filely were notorious, and it wasn't uncommon for bodies washed out to sea to never be recovered. She just hoped they didn't waste too many man hours searching for her. She needed to look online tomorrow and check. Something else to add to her growing to-do list.

But now, the only thing she could do to help Vicky was pray. And that she could do.

Amy sat on a kitchen stool, watching Dane fuss around the girls. Anyone would think he'd never left them before. Well, technically he hadn't, at least not with her. She shot him what she hoped was a reassuring smile. "They'll be fine. And so will I."

"Are you sure? I can ring in, take the day off."

"And do what?" she asked, keeping her tone light. "Watch me Hoover? The girls will be at school until three fifteen or so. Then it's only a couple of hours until you get back."

"OK." He took a deep breath. "I'll cook when I get in."

"OK."

Dane pulled out his keys and slid one off the ring. "I meant to give you this yesterday. It's the front door key."

"Thank you."

He nodded and kissed the girls' foreheads. "Be good. See you tonight."

"Bye, Dad," Jodie answered as he headed out. Then she looked at Amy and pushed the bowl away. "Not hungry."

"That's fine." Amy grimaced as she swallowed the unsweetened coffee.

"You're not going to make me eat?" Jodie sounded surprised.

"I can feed you like a baby if you want, but it won't help. You'll be hungry by lunch if you don't eat, but that's up to you."

"Oh." Jodie's eyes widened. "Dad yells at me until I eat all of it."

"I'm not your dad. But I can yell if you want." She winked as Jodie shook her head. "Now, if you don't like that, then I can pick up something else for breakfast on my way home from school. Personally, if I eat breakfast, then it's muesli."

"Yuk. That's rabbit food." Jodie pulled a face.

Amy was amused to see the look mirrored on Vicky's face. "I thought they ate salad. Anyway, given a choice what would you eat for breakfast? Crackers, a different cereal, toast, eggs, waffles, full English with black pudding..."

"What's black pudding?"

"Cooked dried blood." Amy grinned. "My Dad loved it."

Both girls scrunched up their noses.

Amy laughed. "OK, no black pudding."

"Mum used to get honey loops. Dad won't buy them. He says they are too sweet and bad for us."

"They can be if you eat nothing else besides. Would you eat them if I got them?"

"Yeah."

"OK." Amy looked at Vicky. "Do you like them?"

Jodie answered for her. "She likes toast with marmite and marmalade on."

"At the same time? That sounds..."

"Disgusting?" Jodie nodded. "It's revolting, but yeah. Marmite first, then marmalade."

"I was going to say interesting, but sure I can make that." She looked at Vicky. "Would you rather that instead of cornflakes?"

Vicky pushed the bowl towards her.

Amy smiled and took it away. She put the toast on and glanced at Jodie's cold oatmeal. "That would taste better warmed up with syrup on it."

"Syrup?"

"About a dessert spoonful I reckon. Or chocolate sauce."

"Isn't that bad for your teeth?"

She tilted her head. "Only if you never clean them." She held her hand out for the bowl. "So which is it to be?"

"Syrup."

By eight fifteen, both girls had eaten, and Jodie had left for school without complaint. Amy didn't suppose it'd last, but it was a start. While Vicky went to get her bag and coat, Amy grabbed the notepad. Dane had left twenty pounds for any shopping she needed. Thinking quickly, she wrote cereal. Then she added sugar, as she really couldn't continue to drink tea or coffee without it, pop-up linen bins for the girls' rooms, and fruit.

Vicky came back into the room.

"You got everything?"

A slight nod came in response.

"Cool. Then let's go."

❧❦

Amy dropped Vicky off and then went straight to the library. She logged onto one of the computers and did a search for fake ID. Surprisingly, the search yielded hundreds of results. Prices ranged from ridiculously cheap to ludicrously expensive. Most sites wanted online payment, but there was one based in the UK, which took cash only. She printed off the application form and filled it in. Now all she needed was a passport photo which she could get from the photo booth on the other side of the library. The site promised the card would come within five to seven days, which should be plenty of time.

Photos done, she sealed the envelope and posted

it. Amy pushed down the feelings of guilt. What else could she do?

If there was another way, Lord, I'd take it, but there isn't. This Saunders bloke wants me dead, and I can't go to the police. Right now, I'm here and hoping You led me here for a reason and that's to help this family. Is this You making some good come out of my breaking the law?

Having grocery shopped, she headed back to the house and deactivated the alarm. She put the shopping away and made tea. Half-way around the supermarket, she'd remembered what else she'd meant to do on line. She wanted to check for her name in the news. To see if anything had been said, and if so, what was happening. It wouldn't take long and Dane had said she could use his laptop. She'd do a mega-quick check, then delete her search history. Just in case.

She took the mug into the lounge and fired up the laptop. Sipping the tea, she looked at the main news. There was nothing on the national news pages and only a couple of paragraphs on the local news. The local paper had more information and her picture.

Her photo, detailing the accident and court case took up the top of the page. Then in less detail was the damage to her house and the fact everything had been left on the beach, sparking a full scale rescue. This had now been called off. She was missing, presumed dead. There were short quotes from Ray and Rosalie. A memorial service was being planned for a later date.

Missing, presumed dead.

Her stomach twisted. She hadn't expected it to hurt like this. It was what she wanted, what she'd intended, but it was all so very real now. For an instant, she had the crazy idea of turning up at the memorial.

After all, how many people got to go to their own funeral? But then common sense prevailed.

She finished her tea and stood. First order of business today was to tackle Jodie's room and get rid of the rubbish and dirty laundry. Then to work out how to use the washing machine and set it going on what was likely to be the first of several loads.

The room was worse than it appeared on first sight. It took the best part of three hours to bag up the rubbish and clothes from the floor and under the bed. She finished by hoovering and dusting and opening the windows to let in some fresh air.

There were four loads of washing from that room alone. Never mind doing the bedding as well.

Stopping for a quick bite to eat, Amy spent the time after lunch tidying Jodie's chest of drawers and folding and rearranging everything. Notes stuck on each drawer, told Jodie what went where, although she doubted half this stuff would actually fit anymore.

The clock in the hall struck three and Amy set off to collect Vicky from school. At first it felt weird standing in the playground with all the mothers, but no doubt she would get used to it in time and it would get easier. No one spoke to her; in fact it all seemed rather cliquey.

Vicky plodded over to her, her shoulders slumped and eyes downcast.

Amy smiled in greeting. "Hey, Vicky. Did you have a good day?"

She shook her head, scuffing her shoes on the ground.

"I'm sorry. Would milk and cookies help?"

She shook her head again, slowly heading to the gate.

Amy frowned and caught up. "Did you do any painting today?"

There was no response and despite trying several times more on the way home, Vicky wouldn't even look at her. As soon as they got back to the house, Vicky headed up to her room and shut the door.

Amy sighed. Two steps forward and one back...it seemed that what progress she'd made that morning had been wiped out already.

She let Jodie in a few minutes later and watched her run up the stairs, waiting for the outburst she knew would come as soon as Jodie reached her room. She wasn't disappointed.

"Who's been in my room?"

She went to the foot of the stairs. "Something wrong?" she called.

Jodie appeared on the landing. "Where's my stuff? Who's been in my room?"

"I have. Your clothes are washed and either drying, or in the airing cupboard. The rest are folded and organized in the labeled drawers so you know where they are. Feel free to change them around, but you'll find the system works fairly well."

"And my other stuff?"

"The rubbish is gone. I'm assuming you weren't keeping the empty bottles, cans, glasses, and crisp packets for a reason. Everything else is either in boxes under your bed or in the wardrobe. Books are on the bookcase now. There is also a laundry basket in your room for you to put things in when you take them off. Towels will be hung back in the bathroom, is that understood?"

"Or you'll do what?" Jodie stuck her hands on her hips and screwed her face up in disgust.

"Or you can go back to living in a pigsty, and each week you will have less and less stuff and also be given the hoover to clean it yourself."

"You wouldn't dare. Dad won't let you."

"Who do you think put me in charge of your room, your laundry and so on?"

Jodie stamped her foot and raised her voice. "You're not my mother."

"I have no intentions of trying to be. I never knew her, but from what I've learned she was a wonderful lady who loved you, Vicky, and your dad very, very much." Amy sucked in a deep breath. "The only reason your dad hired me is to look after you when he's at work."

"He's *paying* you? But you're living here."

"Yes, he's paying me. The job comes with the room. Because sometimes he has to work nights or early mornings or late. A nanny is simply a live-in babysitter who also does housework and cleaning and does a lot of fun stuff with the kids. Assuming they want to do fun stuff after school and on the holidays, that is."

"Fun stuff like what?" A faint hint of interest sparked in her voice. Not that you could tell by looking at her.

"We could go swimming, go to the park, walking and shopping. I did see an advert for some stables, so maybe we check out riding lessons at some point. We could cook or do homework or all sorts of things you like to do. But you have to work with me here. Your room doesn't have to be spotless. But you'll get a lot less spiders in there if rubbish goes in the bin and clothes don't live on the floor."

There was a moment of hesitation, then Jodie

narrowed her eyes. "I'll try."

"That's all I ask." She lightened her tone. "So I was thinking, do you want to help me cook dinner? I could teach you how to make pork casserole. Surprise your dad by him not having to cook when he gets in."

"OK."

Amy nodded and returned to the kitchen. She didn't suppose every battle would be that easy, or even that she'd won this round, but it was a start.

꒰๑꒱

Dane let himself in. The house smelled wonderful and it was quiet. Was he in the right place? Or had everyone gone out? He hung his coat on the rack on the wall. "Hello?"

Amy appeared from the kitchen, drying her hands on a tea towel. "Hello. How was your day?"

"Busy. I'm sorry I'm late. How did it go today?"

"It went all right. Vicky is in the bath, and Jodie is in the study doing her homework. She and I cooked, and we saved you some."

"You didn't need to do that. I'd intended to do so when I got in."

"I know, but we thought it'd be nice for you to be cooked for, for a change."

"Thank you." He went through to the kitchen, taking in a deep breath. Whatever she'd cooked smelt wonderful. His mouth watered, and his stomach gurgled in anticipation. He picked up the pile of mail and flicked through it. Bill, bill, bill, bill...nothing changed. He sat down, opening them. "So it went all right today then? Did you do much?"

Amy put his dinner in the microwave. "I tided

Jodie's room."

"Oh, I bet that went down like a dose of salts."

Amy put the kettle on. "It did. But she now has carpet on the floor and clothes in the drawer. We'll see how long it lasts."

He raised an eyebrow as the microwave beeped. "I'm impressed."

"Don't be. She wasn't." She brought over his dinner and set in on the bench in front of him. "I shall get Vicky out of the bath."

Dane closed his eyes and said grace. Picking up his fork he started to eat. It was good, far better than anything he'd have made. The sauce was slightly spicy, and he couldn't put a finger on what was different about it.

Jodie came in and stood on the other side of the bench. "Hi, Dad."

He smiled at her. "Hello. How was your day?"

"It went."

"I heard you helped make this."

"Yeah. It was fun." She shifted from one foot to the other, but didn't seem as stressed as normal. No doubt that wouldn't last. "Do you like it?"

"I really do. Trying to figure out what's in the sauce."

"That's Amy's secret ingredient."

He pouted. "So you won't tell me then?"

"No, 'cause if I did it wouldn't be a secret."

"OK, but you'll have to make it again." He took another bite.

Jodie nodded slightly. "Dad…"

Here we go. Didn't think it would last. That was her I've-got-a-complaint voice. He swallowed. "Yes?"

"Amy tided my room."

"I know. She said." He took another bite. The casserole was all the better for not having cooked himself.

"She said that you said she could, but I don't want her to."

He swallowed. "Then you have to tidy it up yourself. She needs to be able to get in there to clean."

"But, Dad, I don't want—"

Dane resisted the urge to snap. "Otherwise she'll keep doing it. It's not hard, Jodie. If you get something out, you put it away when you've finished with it. And if it's dirty—"

She sighed. "I know. I have to put it in the wash."

He nodded. "So how was school?"

"Pretty rubbish." She gave the standard response. "How was work?"

Well, two could play at that game. "Pretty rubbish."

Vicky came in and hugged him. It looked like she'd been crying, but maybe she'd just gotten soap in her eyes.

He pulled her onto his lap and cradled her. "Hey, sweetie. How was your day?"

Vicky shrugged and leaned against him, picking at his sleeve.

Concern gnawed at him. This was unusual, even for her. He glanced over at Amy as she came into the kitchen, then back down at his daughter. "What did you do today? Did you have PE?"

All he got in response was a shrug.

He picked her up and hugged her. "What about drawing? Or music?"

Again a shrug.

Dane looked at Amy.

"She's been like that since I picked her up from school," Amy said. "She went to her room as soon as we got home. She didn't even want milk and cookies."

"That's not like her." He looked at Vicky. "Can I do anything? Would you like me to read to you?"

She shook her head, her bottom lip trembling and her eyes full of tears.

"Not even *Sophie's Tea Party*?"

She shook her head again, clinging to him tightly.

He thought. "OK. Then how about we go and find the children's Bible with the pictures in it. You can pick one of those."

His sweater felt damp now, and he knew from the way her whole body shook that she was crying. Dane bit his lip. His heart ached for her, filling and threatening to break.

I wish there was something I could do, some way to get through to her, to make it better.

He cradled her in his arms and stood, leaving his partly eaten dinner on the bench. "I'll come back for that later."

"OK."

Dane carried Vicky from the kitchen and up the stairs to her room. He set her on the bed and pulled the large Bible from the bookcase. It contained three hundred and sixty-five stories, one for every day of the year, especially illustrated for children. He and Jas had bought it for Vicky when she was a baby. Sitting next to her, he wrapped an arm around her. "Which one would you like?"

Vicky shrugged.

"Then how about I choose one?" He paused. "How about mummy's favorite story? The lost sheep?" He flicked through the pages slowly until he found the story he was looking for. The picture showed a tiny little sheep, lost in a huge wilderness and caught in the brambles.

Vicky leaned against him, running her finger over the picture, yawning, as he read. After a while, the movement stopped, and she leaned heavily against him.

As he finished the story, he looked down. She was almost asleep, her thumb in her mouth. Closing the Bible, he set it to one side and began to pray.

He began with the one Jas had taught both girls, *gentle Jesus meek and mild*, and then carried on from there, pouring out his heart. Tears filled his eyes and slowly ran down his cheeks. He didn't know what to do. Had he done the wrong thing in employing Amy? Should he find another job, or just stay at home with the girls instead?

5

Within a week, Amy felt settled and at home. Her first weekend hadn't been as bad as she'd feared. Dane had taken them all to the local country park and they fed the animals in the petting zoo and the girls wore themselves out on the adventure playground. She'd loved church on Sunday. Everyone she spoke to was friendly, and the preaching was excellent. Her ID had arrived and sat nestled in her purse with her bus pass and library card.

The routine was established with the girls and at least their clothes were ending up in the laundry baskets rather than the floor, even if the bedrooms still looked like a war zone most of the time. No, make that all of the time. Jodie's floor had stayed clear for two days, but was now back to more or less normal, minus the clothes. Vicky was still coming into Amy's room at two o'clock every morning and seemed more down than ever.

Amy was determined find the problem and sort it, preferably without worrying Dane about it. Perhaps she could try the drawing communication with her that the teacher had mentioned the first afternoon. Having researched it on the internet, and seen it used on a TV cop show to good effect, it was definitely worth a go as Vicky liked drawing and was good at it.

After school she sat Jodie and Vicky at the breakfast bar with lots of new pens and paper. "So," she said pulling a sheet over to her. "We're going to try something different tonight. Rather than me asking how your day was, and telling you what I did, we're going to draw it." She picked up a blue pen and drew a stick figure in a skirt doing the shopping, eating lunch, and cleaning. "That's my day. Jodie, what about yours?"

Jodie rolled her eyes and drew a desk with z's coming out of it.

Amy laughed. "Nice one. So you just slept all day. Tell you what, tomorrow I go to school and sleep and you can stay here and cook, clean, and do piles of laundry and ironing."

Jodie grinned and then added netball posts and a maths equation. Then she drew a heart with Mum inside it and a gravestone with the initials JKP across it, flowers and long grass surrounding it.

"I like that. How about we draw her pictures and tomorrow after school we'll go and put them on her grave."

Both girls nodded.

Amy smiled. "Cool. OK, Vicky, how was your day?"

Vicky slowly drew a tree with a tiny figure standing under it, with huge square eyes. Next she drew a very tall person, with hands three times the size they should be reaching for the smaller figure.

The doorbell rang, and Amy went to answer it. The man flashed a gas board ID and asked to read the meter. She unlocked the garage and showed him where it was. He looked at the numbers and wrote on his clipboard. His gaze followed the pipes across the garage to where they disappeared into the house, before he nodded to her and left. Amy locked up again, surprised when he got into a van and drove away. Maybe she was his last call of the day.

By the time she returned to the girls, Vicky had finished. Over the whole top of the picture was a pair of red slanted eyes, with evil eyebrows. Lots of black lines surrounded it. Amy shuddered at the sheer evil that seemed to emanate from it.

Amy pointed to the bigger of the two figures. "Is that you?"

Vicky shook her head.

"Someone from school, then?"

She shrugged.

Amy tried again, this time tapping the eyes looking down on the figures. "And this?"

Vicky pushed the chair back and ran from the room. Footsteps pounded up the stairs, and her bedroom door slammed shut.

Amy looked at Jodie. "Any ideas?"

Jodie shrugged. "Maybe it's the bogeyman."

"You know he isn't real."

"He killed Mum."

Amy shook her head. "No. A bad man killed your mum and he's now locked up, right?"

"Dad says he won't ever get out. He killed a lot of people. The Prime Minister, too. And he tried to kill Auntie Adeline. Uncle Nate and Dad saved her just in time."

"And that's a good thing."

"But they couldn't stop him from killing Mum. Was it something we did wrong? Is God punishing us by taking her away?"

Amy shook her head. What on earth did she say in response to that? "No. I lost my mum when I was ten. She got very sick and went to hospital and never came home. Dad said that God needed her more in heaven than we needed her here. But that didn't seem fair, because I needed her."

Jodie nodded. "Just like we do. What happened?"

"Dad kept working. He was in the army. I got to go all over the world with him, except when he went away to war."

"Is he still in the army now?" Jodie asked.

Amy shook her head. "He died fighting a war in the desert when I was nineteen."

"So you don't have anyone?"

"No. Maybe what my dad said works for your mum, and God had a job for her to do in heaven. But it is nothing you did, or said, or didn't do. God loves you, and Vicky and your Dad. And He always will. We don't understand why things happen sometimes, but have to trust He will work it out for good, just like it says in Romans chapter eight."

"Even the bad stuff?"

"Especially the bad stuff. Because God doesn't make the bad things happen, bad people do. God takes the results of those actions and works them into something good."

"OK."

Amy nodded. "And any time you want to talk more about this, we can."

Jodie nodded. "Dad still cries when he thinks we're sleeping."

She nodded. "I do too sometimes, when I think of my parents and miss them. But I know they're in heaven and I'll see them again one day."

"Just wish I could make him feel better."

"A hug always helps. Even for grownups. Maybe try that the next time he looks sad." Amy stood and put the pictures in a drawer intending to show Dane when he got back from work. "Now, what would you like for dinner?"

"Chips." Jodie immediately gave the usual response.

"That was a silly question, wasn't it? How about toad in the hole instead?"

"With chips."

"Fine, with chips."

Just as she was about to dish up, she got a text from Dane saying he was going to be really late. She covered his and left it on the side of the counter, finally putting it in the fridge before she went to bed at ten.

∞

As always, Vicky woke her at two in the morning, just standing over the bed. Amy got up and put Vicky back into her bed, sitting with her until she was sure the child had settled. She crept out of the room and pulled the door almost closed. Quietly she turned, and walked straight into Dane. She gasped, her hand flying over her mouth to stifle the sound.

"I'm sorry," he said quietly. His hands touched her arms reassuringly and heat shot through her pyjama sleeves. "I didn't mean to startle you. I've not long gotten in and heard footsteps. Is Vicky all right?"

"She's sleepwalking. Just put her back to bed."

"Sleepwalking?" Concern flickered in his eyes, overriding the exhaustion.

Amy nodded.

"I've just made some tea. Want to join me, talk this through?"

"Sure. Let me just grab my robe."

He nodded. "I'll see you down there."

Amy dashed into her room and fastened her robe tightly over her pyjamas, grateful she wasn't wearing something flimsy and see-through. She followed him downstairs and sat at the breakfast bar in the kitchen. The remains of his dinner sat on the plate by the sink. "How was your day?"

"Rough." Dane brought the tea over. "I deal with death on a daily basis, but when it's a child, it's so much harder."

"I can't imagine doing that every day."

Her mind worked quickly, putting together Jodie's comment about Dane saving Adeline just in time and what he'd just said. He must be a medic of some description. Maybe a doctor or paramedic. That would also explain the long hours and shift work. But Amy didn't ask. She daren't ask, because then he'd ask questions in response, and she had no answers. At least none she could honestly give him.

"Some days I hate it and would rather do something else. The worst part about my job, is having to inform the parents and then watch them fall apart. No parent should have to outlive their child." He took a long sip of his tea. "Anyway, that's enough about my day. You said that Vicky sleepwalks?"

"She has since my first night here. She comes in always at the same time, just after two. She stands by the bed, looking at me. I take her back to bed, stay with her until she's settled. She never remembers it in the morning."

"I didn't know."

"Oh, I'm sorry. I assumed you did, so I tried not to disturb you. I would have said something sooner otherwise. Most kids do it at some point and grow out of it." She felt bad and tried to change the subject. "Would you like to see what they did today? I tried something new with them."

"Sure."

"I overheard what Vicky's teacher said about drawing and looked it up. Apparently it's pretty effective, plus it's been used on some of the TV shows I've seen."

He stared at her over his cup. "I thought I said she didn't need counseling."

"It isn't counseling. It's just another way of communicating and it puts both girls on the same level playing field."

"If you say so."

Amy looked at him. "I wouldn't go against your wishes, but this proved rather interesting." She stood and pulled the pictures from the drawer. "So rather than talk about our day, we drew it. This is mine."

Dane looked at the picture and grinned. "You mean you didn't sit down all day watching TV and eating cream cakes?"

Amy laughed. "Nope, that's what I'm planning for tomorrow. The most exciting thing that happened today was the gas man coming to read the meter."

"Wonderful. I should get the bill next week then."

She handed him another picture. "This is Jodie's."

Dane's smile grew. "Sleeping at school. That doesn't surprise me." He ran his finger over the heart, then paused at the gravestone. A slight frown crossed his face. "What's this?"

"She wouldn't elaborate." She handed him the final one. "And this is Vicky's."

His face hardened completely. "You're kidding."

"Nope." She pointed to the tiny figure under the

tree. "That's her. I'm guessing this is someone she's terrified of, possibly someone from school, but she refused to look at me, never mind nod or shake her head. Jodie says the eyes are the bogeyman."

"She would."

"But I think it's more likely her mother's killer."

"She wasn't there," Dane whispered. "None of us were, despite…" He broke off.

"Despite?"

He shook his head. "We're talking about the kids, not me, or the…bloke that killed Jas. Go on."

"I know I'm no expert, but I'd say whatever it is, is hanging over her. Watching her or guiding her every move. Maybe she's scared that if she speaks, he'll find her or take you away, too."

"It's possible. What about this?" He pointed to the other figures. "Huge eyes mean she's feeling trapped and huge hands usually indicate someone's hurting her."

Amy nodded. "I'll keep an eye on her. And I'll keep drawing with her; see if she comes out with anything else."

"Thank you." He didn't question or comment but rather finished his tea in brooding silence, his brow furrowed. "So what have you got planned for tomorrow?"

"Other than watching TV and eating cream cakes?" She grinned. "I thought I'd check out the ladies meeting at the church. It starts around eleven, I think."

"Sounds like a good idea."

She nodded. "What were you going to say just now?" she asked quietly. "None of us were there despite…what?"

Dane took a deep breath, his fingers clenching into

a fist. "It was really horrid. There was a serial killer stalking the streets with several victims already. Adeline, Nate's wife, was having premonitions, and seeing the murders either as they happened, or just before. She'd been there when the Prime Minister was assassinated. She had a vision, described it..." His voice broke. "Only it was Jas. Nate found her body, came and told me. I destroyed the kitchen somewhat."

She glanced around.

"Not this one. We moved about ten months after her death. I couldn't stay there any longer." He sighed. "The girls weren't too keen at first, but I couldn't stand being around somewhere she'd been. This place is probably a lot bigger than we need, but it's mine and the girls seem happy here. They had a lot of say in where the furniture went, what room was painted which color and so on."

"It's a lovely house." She paused. "It must have been a hard time for all of you."

Dane blinked, his eyes glistening. "Yeah, it was." He stood. "Anyway, I should let you get back to bed. Or it'll be time to get up. I'll see to the cups."

Amy took the hint and dropped it. "Yeah, thanks for the tea. Good night."

❧

On the way to the church for the ladies meeting the next morning, she passed the school. It had to be break time as the playground was covered in children playing. She slid her hands into her coat pockets and stood searching for Vicky. Then she saw her.

Vicky stood on her own under a tree very much like the one in her pictures. A child ran over to her, pulling at her sleeve. Perhaps she was trying to get Vicky to join in with the game. Amy looked for a member of staff, but there didn't seem to be anyone on playground duty. At that moment, the bell rang and the children scarpered.

Tears ran down Vicky's face, and she slowly trudged towards the building, while a teacher shouted for her to hurry up.

Not sure what to do, Amy looked at Vicky. Should she go in, take her out of school? She prayed that God would show her what to do and that He'd be with Vicky in class.

Amy glanced at her watch, and headed on towards the church. The meeting was good, and she was glad she'd gone. On the way back, the children were out for lunch. She once again looked for Vicky and it didn't take long to find her.

She was back under the tree. Crying, with several girls around her. Purely because it bore a striking resemblance to what Vicky had drawn, Amy pulled out her phone and took a couple of photos. She'd compare the tree with the drawing later.

Again, there was no sign of any adults around. What if this explained the drawing? Was she being bullied? She'd talk to Vicky as soon they got home, then to her teacher first thing in the morning. Dane would want to know, but he'd been so tired that morning and was so busy at work, she didn't want to call him now and disturb him. Not that she knew what he did for a job.

He could be a government spy or MP or a refuse collector for all she knew. Although most of those were out, especially the bin man, as they didn't work much past midday. Besides, he'd said something about death and children, so, yes, most likely a doctor of some kind. She'd tell him when he came home from work and the girls were in bed.

Vicky refused to even nod or shake her head again on the way home, or even look at Amy as she tried to ask about playtimes.

After school, she sat the girls down at the table. "OK, this afternoon, I covered those cards you did for your mum. I want you to draw me how your day went. Then we're going to go to the cemetery and put the cards on your mum's grave."

"It'll be dark." Jodie shook her head.

"It might start getting dark on the way home, but not if you draw quickly." She started making dinner while the girls drew. Jodie's picture had another gravestone and the initials JKP on it. Again tucked away in the corner of the page, but larger than before. That was rather worrying. Almost as much as the *see you soon* Jodie had written on the card for her mum.

Vicky's picture was the tree with four huge figures surrounding a much smaller person. And the tree was the same as the one at school.

Amy slid the cards into her bag, and handed the girls their coats. "OK, let's go."

"Can we get flowers, too?" Jodie asked. "Mum liked daisies."

"Sure, we can do that."

They caught the bus to the small cemetery on the other side of town, and bought the flowers from the shop at the bottom of the road. The girls knew where the grave was, and Amy stood to one side, giving them some privacy. She took a close look at the gravestone. It wasn't the one Jodie kept drawing. She checked her watch. "We should start to head back in a minute."

The girls nodded.

After a couple more minutes, it began to drizzle. "Time to go. We can return another day." She took Vicky's hand and started walking towards the main road.

Vicky tugged her hand and pointed to the swings across the road.

Amy nodded. "Just a few minutes. Don't want to get too wet."

"We'll be late," Jodie complained.

"So we get back after your dad. Is that going to be a problem?"

"He'll worry."

"I'll text him." They crossed the road by the lights and entered the park. Vicky ran on ahead to the swings.

"Can I do it?" Jodie held out her hand for the phone.

"OK." Amy gave her the phone and started pushing Vicky.

Jodie played with the phone, sitting on an empty swing, with her arms wrapped around the chains. "You got a text. Can I open it?"

Amy nodded. It would only be Dane anyway, as no one else had the number.

"Dad says, *where are you? I'll pick you up on my way home.*" Jodie didn't return her phone but typed quickly. "Memorial Park. The cemetery side by the swings." She grinned. "How many kisses?"

"None."

"That's six then."

"No—" Surely Jodie hadn't added hugs and kisses to a text Dane would assume came from Amy.

"Too late." Jodie laughed and handed back the

phone. "Can you push both of us?"

"I can try." Amy pushed both swings, desperately hoping Jodie was teasing about the kisses.

Not more than ten minutes later, Dane stomped over to them, his face set and his eyes dark and glittering. His whole body resonated anger.

Vicky jumped off the swing and ran to him.

He picked her up and held out a hand to Jodie. "Let's go."

Jodie nodded and took his hand, walking with him back to where he'd left the car.

Amy stood there. Was it something she'd done? Maybe she'd done the wrong thing in coming out with them. Should she follow or stay here?

Dane glanced over his shoulder. "Come on," he said in a don't-mess-with-me tone.

Amy followed slowly.

He didn't speak to her the entire drive home. Dinner was just as silent, not even Jodie dared say anything. Dane sat there, seething as he ate. Finally, he stood and beckoned to Vicky. "Bedtime."

Amy watched him exit the room with Vicky and sighed. Leaving the dishes where they were, she put on her coat and went for a walk in the rain. She liked it here. She loved the kids, and the way Dane interacted with them, no matter how tired he was. She just wished she knew what she'd done.

ȣ❤ȣ

Dane sat in the lounge. He'd put the girls to bed and come down to talk to Amy to find her gone. Not even a note. On the plus side, she'd only taken her bag and coat, so he was hopeful that she would be back at some point. Did he text her? Or did he leave it a little longer? He closed his eyes and rubbed the back of his neck. It had been a lousy day, and he really didn't need this on top of everything else. Finally, the front door opened and closed. Footsteps crossed the hall. He stood and walked to the doorway. "Amy, can I have a word?"

Her hair stuck to her head in rat's tails, dripping onto her shoulders. "Can I just change first? It's chucking it down out there, and my coat isn't as waterproof as I thought it was. I'll be five minutes."

"OK." He went back into the lounge and put the TV on. He tried to focus on the program, but his mind was too caught up with other things. He drummed his fingers on the arm of the chair, not sure how to say what he needed to. He still felt married. He didn't need the growing attraction to the nanny, never mind any affection she bore towards him, however inappropriate it might be, and he certainly wasn't about to—

Amy came in, wearing a tracksuit that showed off her figure beautifully, towel dried hair falling over her shoulders.

Dane mentally shook himself. Now wasn't the time to be admiring how pretty she was. He couldn't go that route. Couldn't and shouldn't. So why did he want to more than anything?

She sat on the edge of the sofa, her unease apparent. She looked as guilty as her body language indicated. "Did the girls go down all right?"

"Yes."

"That's good."

He drew in a sharp breath. "I understand from Jodie that you took them to the cemetery this afternoon."

Amy swallowed, her fingers lacing and unlacing. "Yes, I did. They made cards. We put them in clear plastic bags and left them on their mum's grave."

"Why?"

"It's obvious both girls miss her a lot." She shifted under his gaze and looked at the floor. Was she hiding something? "I—I thought this way they could at least visit, tell her they love her. Then we went to the park on the way home and you picked us up there."

He nodded, pushing down his irritation. At least her motives had been in the right place. "Yeah. About those texts you sent…"

Amy sighed. "Actually, Jodie sent them while Vicky was on the swings. How many kisses did she put in the end?"

He raised an eyebrow in surprise. "You knew about that?"

"She threatened to do it. I told her no."

"Six."

Amy grimaced. "Sorry."

"Nate found it amusing. My boss didn't."

"I'm sorry."

He sucked in a deep breath, his anger tempered slightly. "The first one had kisses, as well."

Amy shifted in her seat, picking at a fingernail.

He narrowed his eyes. His copper's instinct went on full alert. She was definitely hiding something, but what? Was this going to be Adeline all over again? He knew Nate had had his doubts about her at one point.

"You're my employer," she said finally. "I wouldn't do that."

"OK." He dropped it. "Did you do any more drawing with them?"

"Yeah. I'll get them." She got up and left the room.

Dane picked up the TV remote and changed channels, putting the football on. Maybe this would take his mind off things for a while.

Amy returned and held out two pieces of paper. "Here."

Dane took them and studied them. Concern gnawed at him and goose bumps rose on his skin. Both pictures scared him. Maybe the girls did need to see a doctor or a psychologist. He pinched the bridge of his nose.

"What I find interesting is Jodie's."

He jerked his head up to look at her. "Interesting?" That was so not the word he'd have used to describe it.

"Yeah. That's not her mother's grave in the picture. And each time she draws it, it's bigger than before."

"It's her initials. Jodie Kathlyn Philips." He looked at the picture. Had he missed something? She seemed fine outwardly, coping at least better than Vicky was, and to some extent better than him. But this? This was way out of his comfort zone, and he had no idea what to do. "What is she trying to tell us? That she wants to die?"

"I don't think so. But she is worried about dying and death." She paused for a moment. "All teenagers feel worthless at some point. All those hormones kick in and they don't know whether they are coming or going. Maybe this is her way of expressing it."

He didn't bother to point out again that Jodie wasn't a teenager, but twelve. "But what if it isn't? What if she's self-harming or something?"

"She's too fond of those very short strappy tops, and I haven't seen any signs of it. But I'll keep an eye out."

"Thank you." He took a deep breath. "And the next time you want to take them to the cemetery, let me know, and I'll drive you all over there. It's not the best part of town to be in after dark."

"OK. I'm sorry."

He nodded. A sudden cheer from the TV distracted him, and he glanced up to watch the replay of the goal. "Good one. About time Reading scored an away goal." He paused. "Do you mind if I keep this on? I could do with the distraction tonight."

"Not at all. I did want to mention something. I walked by the school twice today and Vicky was crying both times."

"The teacher says Vicky is constantly crying, but I'll speak to her teacher." He stifled a sigh. It wasn't just his boss who evidently thought he was a bad parent. From the constant comments from her teacher, she probably did as well. And when he did try to ask about things at school, the blame was put on Vicky's inability to talk.

There was silence for a minute then Amy stood. "I'll see you in the morning. I have some stuff to do upstairs."

"OK. Good night." He leaned back heavily in the chair as she left and closed his eyes. *Well that went well. Nice one. Managed to mess that up good and proper.* He reviewed his reaction to the texts he'd received. They'd been flippant, teasing, almost flirty and those kisses? He should have known she wouldn't have sent them. It was now obvious it was Jodie, but at the time?

Get over it. Amy's a lot younger than you. You're an old man, Dane. End of.

He looked at the photo on the sideboard of him, Jas and the kids. He would die alone and probably, like his grandmother, be widowed longer than he was married in the first place. Love was what he had felt for his wife. Not his children's nanny. What he felt for her was—

He paused. He wasn't sure. He liked having her around. Liked having someone to talk to in the evenings and to be with rather than sitting alone.

OK, I admit it. There is something there. Something there shouldn't be.

Infatuation, he decided. Nothing more. Nothing that would be returned. No matter what he thought or hoped or anything else for that matter.

A loud crash echoed from the kitchen. A short cry of pain, cut off. He leapt to his feet and ran the short distance across the hall.

Amy stood by the sink, a bloody tea towel clamped over her wrist. She was shaking, her wide brown eyes staring and haunted, and more worrying than anything else, she had no color whatsoever.

6

"What happened?" Dane ran over to Amy and gently guided her to the stool.

She kept shaking. "Just being an idiot. I jumped at my own reflection and dropped a glass into the sink. It shattered and cut my wrist."

"Let me see." He gently lifted the tea towel and grimaced, his stomach turning. The cut was deep and gushing. He put the towel back and applied firm pressure to it, raising her arm above her head. "We need to get you to the ED, now."

"No." Her response was too fast for his liking. Her eyes closed and then reopened.

"Why not? This needs stitches."

"It means waking the girls and taking them."

"That's not a problem."

She shook her head, abject terror written in her eyes. She shuddered hard, but that was probably from shock rather than fear. "Please, I don't like hospitals."

The towel oozed beneath his fingers. He grabbed another one, wrapping it tightly over the first, not liking the amount of blood she was losing and the speed at which this was happening. "You need stiches." He reached into his pocket and pulled out his phone. He'd ring the doc attached to the station as police surgeon and beg a favor. If Janice couldn't come out, then he'd take Amy in, whether she liked it or not.

Janice answered the phone on the second ring. As a doctor, he imagined she was used to being on call. Something he could never do—the doctoring bit, not the being on call. First aid was his limit of medical knowledge. "Hello."

"Hi, Janice, it's Dane. Sorry to ring so late."

The tiredness vanished from her voice. "It's not late, not by my standards anyway. What's up? Do you need me at the station?"

"No, but I do need a favor. My kids' nanny has cut her wrist pretty badly and has a morbid fear of hospitals. I don't suppose there is any chance you could come and take a look? It'll need stitching most likely."

"For you, sure. I'm on my way."

❧

Amy sat in the kitchen as Dane showed the doctor out. He seemed really friendly with her, which was good, because she didn't stand a chance with him, no matter what direction her thoughts took at times. She looked at her bandaged wrist. It had been a close call, in more ways than one. She was stupid. She'd seen a figure in the window and thought it was *him*. But it had been her reflection. It was her fault for not closing the blind when it had gotten dark. But she liked the way the solar lights lit the edge of the pond and twinkled its reflection.

She ran her fingers over the bandage. It was bloodstained already. She had to go to the doctor's in the morning and get the stiches checked and the wound redressed. She'd argued that she didn't have a GP yet, but the woman, Dr. Janice Chandler, had said she could go and see her at the end of morning surgery and wouldn't need an appointment.

She reached over and pulled the blind down over the window.

Dane came back in. "How are you doing?"

"OK," she whispered closing her eyes. In reality, she felt cold and sick and light-headed, but if she mentioned that, he'd have her on the way to the ED and then the game would be up. He'd know who she was and send her away.

Dane's voice came from a long way off and echoed. "Amy?"

"Really tired..." she managed. "Might go to bed." She stood to find her legs buckle underneath her.

Just before she fell, strong arms surrounded her and she was enveloped in clouds of Dane's aftershave. She leaned against his chest, hearing his heart beat in time with hers as he carried her up the stairs and into her room. He laid her on the bed and sat by her. His voice still echoed. Why was he speaking from so far away? She struggled to focus on his voice.

"I should have taken you to the ED. Maybe I still should."

"No," she managed. "Your friend fixed it."

"You've lost a lot of blood."

Blood...

A squeal of brakes and a series of three loud thuds —bumper, bonnet, and windscreen. The glass cracked, blood streaked the windscreen and the road...

Amy jumped, her heart pounding and thudding in her ears. "I didn't mean it..."

Dane's warm fingers cradled her face, pushing the hair from her eyes. "Hey, where did you go?"

"Hmmm?"

"You zoned out on me. Said you didn't mean to do it?"

Her cheeks burned. "Cut myself," she whispered. "I didn't mean to break the glass either. I'm sorry."

"Accidents happen. Get some sleep."

She nodded, closing her eyes, a shaft of grief stabbing her as he moved his hand and got up. She tugged the covers around her, drifting in and out of sleep until a shadow appeared in front of her. She jerked awake to find Vicky standing by the bed, eyes wide. Amy reached out a hand for her.

Vicky backed away, screaming, and waving her arms.

Amy threw the covers back, reaching for Vicky. "It's OK, sweetie."

Vicky kept screaming.

Dane ran into the room. "What's going on?"

Amy shook her head. "I don't know. I woke, and she was there. I reached for her, and she flipped. She's never done this before."

Dane gently wrapped his arms around Vicky, sitting on the edge of the bed and cradling her. "It's all right, sweetheart. Daddy's here. You're safe now."

Vicky clung to him, sobbing.

Dane rubbed her back, whispering to her.

"I'm sorry," Amy whispered. "I must have scared her somehow or woken her."

"Don't be sorry. At least we know her voice still works."

"Dad..." Jodie appeared in the doorway. "Is she all right?"

"Vicky's fine, honey," Dane said. "She just had a nightmare. Go back to bed. I'll come see you once she's settled."

Jodie yawned and rubbed her eyes. "OK." She turned and wandered back down the hallway.

Dane hugged Vicky. "Did something scare you, honey?"

Vicky pointed to Amy's bloodied bandage.

Amy felt sick. This *was* her fault. "I'm sorry. I cut myself. But it's OK. Daddy got a doctor out and she fixed me."

Vicky shook her head.

Dane hugged her. "Sweetie, I promise. Amy's going to be just fine. It's a small cut. Dr. Janice fixed it."

She looked at him and frowned slightly.

"Daddy's doctor friend from work, remember? I took you to see her when you had an earache last summer. She gave you some drops and some banana medicine to stop the hurting."

She nodded slightly.

"So when Amy broke a glass and cut herself, I called Dr. Janice. She came out and looked at Amy's wrist. She made it better. I promise. Amy will be just fine."

Amy reached out a hand and rubbed Vicky's fingers. "Do you want to sleep in here tonight?"

Dane frowned and raised an eyebrow.

Amy looked at him. "That way she can make sure I'm all right and it's just tonight."

Vicky nodded, sliding under the covers beside her.

"OK, but just this once." Dane tucked her in and kissed her forehead. "Night, sweetie."

Vicky pointed to Amy.

Dane chuckled. "No, I'm not going to kiss Amy goodnight or tuck her in. She's already tucked in quite nicely."

Amy pretended to pout.

Dane grinned. "Goodnight." He headed out and shut the door.

Amy turned onto her side and looked at Vicky. "Want me to leave the light on?"

Vicky nodded. She took tight hold of Amy's hand and closed her eyes.

৵৽

Dane came into the kitchen, his mind going over the events of the night before. Both girls were dressed and at the table, eating. He did a double take. Up, dressed, *and* eating? Was Amy some kind of miracle worker? He peered at Jodie's bowl. That wasn't oatmeal. "What have you got?" he asked.

"Honey circle things," Jodie said. "Vicky has jam, marmite, and marmalade on the same piece of toast."

Oh, yuk. That is even more disgusting than before. He raised an eyebrow. "Really?"

Jodie mimicked his gesture. "Yes, really. And we got chocolate milk. With a straw."

Dane looked at Amy. "Sweet stuff? I thought we'd had the conversation about that."

"They've promised to clean their teeth afterwards. The straw means the milk doesn't touch their teeth and they're eating without a fuss."

"What about you?" he asked, noting there wasn't a plate in front of her.

"She always eats without a fuss," Jodie said. "Amy's a girly swot."

Amy looked shocked as she reached for the toast. "I'm a *what*?"

"Girly swot, nerd, teacher's pet, goody two shoes…"

"I know what one is, thank you." Amy poked her good naturedly. "I just didn't think that eating breakfast made me one."

"Why do you think we don't usually eat?" Jodie laughed.

Amy winked. "I thought that was just to wind your Dad up."

"Well, there is that as well. But mainly because we don't want to be girly swots."

Dane chuckled, grabbing the last piece of toast. "Does that make me one as well?"

Vicky nodded slowly.

He sat down. "And you're a cheeky monkey." He reached for the butter, glancing at Amy, concern filling him. She looked pale and gaunt. Had she slept at all after Vicky woke her? "Are you OK? I can call in to work, and take the day off if you need me to."

She shook her head. "I'm fine. It's a small cut, nothing more. Once the girls are at school, I can rest. And I've got that doctor's appointment for it, anyway."

"OK, see that you do. And if you do need me, call or text and I'll come home. I'll cook tonight."

"OK."

Jodie looked at Amy over the top of her glass. "Can we go to the park after school, Amy? We can go to the one down the road. It's huge. Have you been there yet?"

"No, I haven't. And sure. Does it have a duck pond?"

Vicky nodded, her eyes lighting up.

"Then I'll bring bread for the ducks. We could go straight from school. If that's all right with your dad."

Dane nodded.

"Can Vianne come?"

"So long as it's all right with her parents."

"She lives with her uncle and aunt. Can she stay for dinner, too?"

Dane looked at Amy. "That's my partner Nate and his wife Adeline."

"Ah. I met Adeline properly yesterday. Vicky's drawing underestimated the cuteness of her hearing dog."

Dane nodded. "Actually, maybe we have them all over to dinner tonight." He pulled out his phone and texted Nate. Within a few seconds he got a reply. "They'd love to. Vianne is to come straight here from school with you, Jodie. Nate suggests we get take-out on the way home from work. I'm going to pick him up, and Adeline will bring his car over this afternoon when she finishes work."

"Can we have fish and chips?" Jodie asked.

He tilted his head. "I was thinking Chinese, but sure, you kids can have fish and chips." He turned to Amy. "Are you sure you're going to be OK?"

Amy sighed and rolled her eyes. "Yes, Daddy."

Jodie squealed with laughter and even Vicky smiled.

Dane grinned. "Good. Don't forget the doctor's either. You need the dressing changed." He kissed the girls, and put his plate in the sink.

It made such a difference knowing the girls were in good hands and happy. Not that they weren't with his parents or Jas's parents, but Amy was different. She'd done more in a few days, than anyone else had accomplished since they'd lost their mum.

And that, he decided, was more than a miracle. It was an answer to prayer.

৵৵৽

Amy tidied the kitchen as the girls grabbed their school bags and jackets. It was so nice being part of this family. If only it were her own. A man who loved her, who looked after his kids the way Dane cared for his, was all she wanted. Since Rosalie had found Ray, she'd been looking, but no one had caught her eye. Or rather, she hadn't caught anyone else's eye.

If she ever found a man like Dane, she would willingly give him kids, something she'd never really wanted for herself until now. She paused. What she really wanted was this family. To be part of Dane's life…

Her heart skipped a beat whenever he entered the room. When he'd been mad at her the previous evening, her heart had almost broken, and then sang when he cared for her when she cut her wrist. His touch had turned her to jelly and burned through her.

Her face grew hot at the thought of him carrying her, his breath on her neck and his fingers pushing her hair behind her ears. Ray had looked at Rosalie the same way.

But now Amy was going too far. She was Dane's nanny, well his daughters' nanny, nothing more.

Vicky tugged at her hand, dragging her back to reality.

"Yes, I'm coming. Are you ready?"

Vicky nodded, holding up her bag.

"Then let's go." She slid the envelope on the counter into her handbag and glanced around. "Where's my phone?"

Vicky grinned and pointed to the bread bin.

"What's it doing there? Trying to hide from me,

you say?" Amy asked.

Vicky shrugged, still smiling.

Amy put her phone in her bag. "There, now try to run away. OK, now we can go."

She took Vicky's hand and set the alarm before leaving the house. She took Vicky into the classroom, rather than leaving her in the playground as usual. She glanced around, taking in the colorful displays of children's work and the swarm of children in navy blue uniforms.

"Miss Stabler. Is everything OK?" Miss Macnin came over to her. "We don't encourage caregivers to come into school with the children. Mr. Philips should have made you aware of that."

"No, everything's not all right. Yesterday as I was passing by, I saw Vicky crying in the playground, the second time she was surrounded by a group of girls who were saying things to her, making her cry. I want something done about it."

"Did you hear what they were saying?"

"No, but—"

"Maybe they simply wanted her to join in. She's not the easiest of children. She's more of a loner."

"What if they weren't asking her to play with them? Do you know for sure? I couldn't see an adult anywhere on the playground."

"I don't really have time right now to discuss Vicky's inability to join in with the other children at break time." The teacher dodged three of the children. "Come and see me tonight."

Amy stood there, about to argue. Was she being brushed off? Did no one but her care what was going on here?

The teacher turned away, clapping her hands.

"Everyone on the carpet for registration, now."

Amy slowly headed from the classroom and stood in the hallway. So, how did she get to the head's office from here?

A woman wearing an ID badge on looked at her. "Can I help you?"

"I need to speak with the head teacher. I'm not sure which way to go."

"It's down this way."

Amy followed the woman through the hallways to the office. "Thank you." She looked at the receptionist. "I'd like to see the head teacher please."

"And you are?"

"Miss Stabler. It's in connection with Vicky Philips. I'm her nanny."

The receptionist vanished, and Amy turned to look at the notices and staff photo board. She hadn't realized the school employed so many teachers and teaching assistants.

"Miss Stabler?" The voice was deep, with the hint of an accent, almost at odds with the very tall, blond man who stood before her. His glasses perched on the end of his nose, and along with his suit, offered the picture of professionalism. "I'm Garth Tovey, head of Headley Cross Primary. How can I help you?"

She took the offered hand and shook it. "I'm Vicky Philips's nanny. I was wondering if I could talk to you about her for a few minutes."

"Sure. Come into my office." He led her two doors down the corridor and shut the door. "Have a seat."

Amy sat at the huge oval table that filled the room.

"Is there a problem with Vicky?"

"For the past week I've been doing a drawing therapy with her. As she won't speak, we communicate by drawing instead."

"I've heard of it. It's meant to give good results."

Amy nodded. She pulled the envelope from her bag. "She always draws herself under the tree with a bigger person standing over her with huge hands. This is last night's." She pulled out the picture and showed him. "As you can see this time there are four others around her. Yesterday morning I happened to be passing the school at break time and saw Vicky standing under the tree crying. Then on the way back, it was lunch time. She was still under the tree crying without an adult in sight and there were four girls talking to her. I don't think they were trying to get her to play with them."

"Could you identify any of the other girls?"

"I have a couple of photos I took yesterday." Amy passed him her phone. "I took them because I wanted to compare the tree in her drawings to the one here. There were no staff members on the playground that I could see on either occasion."

He glanced up sharply. "I will also look into that. There should have been at least two people there." He scribbled names down on a piece of paper handed Amy back her phone. He pressed a button on the intercom. "Helen, can you bring Vicky Philips from 1M to my office, please?"

Minutes later, the door opened and Vicky came in slowly, with wide eyes. The color drained from her face as she saw Amy sitting there.

Amy held out a hand to her. "It's all right, sweetheart. You're not in trouble."

Vicky slowly went over to her, perching on the edge of the chair next to her.

Mr. Tovey looked at her. "Miss Stabler tells me

you've been talking to her through your drawings."

Vicky nodded.

"She also tells me you've been having a few problems on the playground."

Vicky looked at Amy, her eyes wide and her mouth open in horror.

Mr. Tovey pushed over a pad of paper and a pen. "Can you show me what happens in the playground, Vicky?"

Vicky hesitated for a moment then leaned over the paper. Her tongue hovered over her bottom lip as she painstakingly drew a tree and several stick figures. As she continued, her sleeve slid up her arm, revealing the bruises underneath it.

Mr. Tovey looked at Vicky. "You really should have come and seen me or Miss Macnin, when this first began happening. We could have stopped it."

She shook her head, wrapping her arms around her middle.

"You go back to class, and I'll speak to the girls in the photo."

Vicky shook her head again, looking at Amy and then pointed to the window.

"Sweetheart, I can't take you home," Amy said, assuming that's what she wanted. "But I'll be waiting for you at the end of the day. I promise. And we're doing something fun on the way home, remember?" She hugged her tightly. "We're picking up Jodie and Vianne and going to the park, aren't we?"

Vicky nodded. She hugged her back, then slowly left the room.

Amy looked at Mr. Tovey. "You'll put a stop to this?"

"I'll certainly speak to the girls responsible.

Bullying isn't acceptable in any shape or form. Thank you for bringing it to my attention. May I have a copy of the photos?"

"I'll be glad to forward them," Amy said. "I'll be speaking to her father tonight. He'll be glad to know it's dealt with. Thank you."

7

Dane changed gear and glanced at Nate. The morning had been a total waste of time. What they thought had been a lead had turned into a dead end. "Now what?"

Nate shook his head. "I have no idea. I wish I did." He leaned back in his seat, looking out the window. "Hey, isn't that your nanny sitting over there opposite the school?"

"Yeah—wonder what's up. I won't be a sec." Dane pulled over and parked the car. He got out and walked across the pavement to Amy. He took a seat on the bench next to her. "You can take watching the girls too far," he joked.

Amy glanced at him. "Hi, Dane."

His heart warmed at her use of his name. There was something about the way she said it, that was different from everyone else. "Aren't you meant to be resting? How's your wrist?"

"Sore." Her gaze darted back to the playground. "But I'll live."

"Did you get to the doctor's, to have the dressing changed?"

"No, something more important cropped up. Dane, I had something to tell you last night, but I wanted to wait for a good time, then I cut my wrist and..." She peeked around him, trying to keep her eyes on the playground.

He touched her arm, concerned. "Are you really OK? You seem distracted."

"Not really. Watching Vicky."

Dane looked over at the playground. It was heaving with children running here and there, the screams and laughter reaching them from across the road. "Where is she?"

"She's under the tree on the left." She handed him her phone. "Yesterday, as I was walking back to your house from the church, I saw her under the tree crying. It looked like the one from her drawings. It could simply be like her teacher said and the kids were trying to get her to play."

Dane looked at the photos and beckoned Nate over. "But?"

"Something didn't seem right. I spoke to the head teacher this morning, and he called Vicky in. She has bruises on her arms. The head said he'd deal with it. I wanted to sit here and make sure it was sorted." She glanced up as Nate stood behind them, looking at the photos over Dane's shoulder.

His fingers clenched into fists as he struggled with the rage filling him. How could he not have known something was wrong? How did he miss something as important as this? He shrugged off Nate's calming hand, knowing Nate would react the same way if it were Vianne that was being hurt. As he watched the playground, four girls went over to Vicky and surrounded her. He scowled. "Sorted it, right..."

Then he leapt to his feet as they laid into her. "Nate..." He checked the road before launching across it, with Nate and Amy close behind him.

"Leave her alone!" he roared.

Amy rang the bell on the gate.

Dane watched in despair. The girls kept laying into Vicky, seemingly oblivious to everything around them. He looked for the adult on duty, but there was no one in sight.

"Hello?" A voice crackled through the speaker on the gate.

Amy leaned into it. "This is—"

Dane shook his head. He didn't have time for niceties. "This is DS Philips and DS Holmes. There's an assault in progress on the playground. I need you to let us in now."

Nothing happened. "Amy, stay here and keep trying. Nate, with me."

"Where are you...?" Amy began then turned back to the intercom.

Dane scaled the fence and vaulted over it quickly; knowing Nate would be right behind him. Landing on his feet, he charged toward the tree. "Get away from her!" he yelled.

Vicky cowered, with her arms over her head.

The children around her scattered, but Nate set off in pursuit, catching them.

Dane reached Vicky and crouched beside his distraught daughter. He wrapped his arms tightly around her. "It's OK, honey. Daddy's here, now."

Vicky sobbed, her whole body shaking uncontrollably, as she clung to him.

Three teachers, Mr. Tovey, and Amy converged on the scene. Another teacher blew the whistle three times and got all the other children to line up in classes.

Talk about shutting the stable door after the horse had bolted.

Dane's anger flowed from him without restraint. "I was told this had been sorted," he said furiously. "I did not expect to see it happening again. Why wasn't anyone out here on playground duty?"

"There should have been," Mr. Tovey said. "I spoke to the girls this morning, but that obviously wasn't enough."

"Obviously," Dane muttered, not hiding the sarcasm.

Nate put a hand on his shoulder. "Can we take this inside?" he said. "Away from all the other kids?"

Mr. Tovey nodded. He turned to a tall blonde woman. "Emma, take those four inside and sit them outside my office and ring their parents please. I need them all to come in—drag them out of work if need be. I'll take Vicky to the school nurse to check her over."

"That's not necessary," Dane said sharply. At this point he didn't trust anyone from the school with his daughter. "I'll arrange a medical checkup myself." He stood with Vicky still in his arms, following the head teacher inside the school building. They all headed down to the head teacher's office. "Amy will take her home."

Vicky shook, still clinging to him, as he sat on one of the chairs around the large oval table.

Dane kissed her forehead. "Honey, Daddy is going to stay here and make sure this doesn't happen again. I want you somewhere safe and right now that's at home with Amy." He glanced at Nate, who nodded. "Uncle Nate agrees. Actually..." He pulled out his phone and hit speed dial. It answered on the second ring. "Guv, its Dane. I need two patrol cars to Headley Cross Primary, now."

"What's up?"

"Assault. Four kids attacked Vicky, and it's not the first time from what I understand."

"You want to arrest a bunch of six-year-olds?" DI Welsh sounded incredulous.

"These kids aren't six, but I have something else in mind. And I know better than to talk to the kids involved myself."

"Is Vicky OK?"

"She's shaken, scared, and it's hard to tell if she's injured or not here. I just want her home. Amy doesn't drive, and Nate and I only have the pool car here."

"Sure. Two cars on the way. Come and see me when you get back. I'll need you both to bring me up to speed and fill out a report."

"Thanks, Guv. Will do." He hung up. "Vicky, honey, a uniformed officer is going to come and take you and Amy home. You'll be safe there."

She didn't let go.

"I promise." He hugged her. "And it won't be long before I'm home. And don't forget Uncle Nate, Auntie Adeline, and Vianne are coming for dinner tonight."

She looked up slowly.

"Bringing chips," Nate added.

"I need your help to make a pudding," Amy said. She had as little color in her cheeks as Vicky did. "Maybe we make a chocolate one."

Dane hugged her. "She said the C word," he whispered, finally getting a slight smile from his daughter. "But I'll pretend I didn't hear that."

Two police cars with blue lights flashing pulled up outside the windows.

Mr. Tovey looked at him. "Isn't that a little overkill?"

Dane stiffened. "What would you do if it were your daughter?" he asked. "And I have no intentions of speaking to those girls myself. That is what the uniformed officers are for. Besides, you had two police officers witness the assault, from outside the school this time. There is no way this is now an in-house problem."

He looked at Vicky. "Let's get you and Amy out of here and then Daddy can sort things out here." He glanced up. "I'll be right back." He stood and took Vicky's hand, leading her out to reception.

Four tall uniformed officers stood there. He nodded to them. "Ben, can you take Vicky and Amy home and then come back here and help me?"

The officer nodded. "Sure, Sarge." He winked at Vicky. "Would you like the flashing lights on all the way to your house?" he asked in a stage whisper. "Just don't tell the Sarge."

Vicky nodded shyly, taking hold of Amy's hand.

Dane looked at Amy. "I won't be late tonight. Just keep an eye on her, make sure she's not hurt in anyway. If she is, text me, and I'll get Janice over to check her out."

"OK." Amy nodded, her voice wobbling slightly.

Dane studied her and caught hold of her arm. He didn't like how pale she was. "Are you all right? Is the cut aching? You seem a little out of sorts."

"I'm fine. You see to things here."

Her appearance belied her words, but now wasn't the time to call her on it. He'd do that later, once the girls were in bed. She must really have come to care for his children if the assault had affected her this much. He nodded, his anger dissipating as his cop side kicked in. Vicky was safe, now he could deal with this. "OK."

He walked them to the door, then turned to look at Nate.

Nate held his gaze. "You can't arrest a bunch of

seven–year-olds. Even if it was full blown assault, in front of police officers. Never mind the photographic evidence of a prior."

"That's what the Guv said, but I don't intend to arrest them."

"What are you planning then?"

Dane looked at him, Mr. Tovey, and the uniformed officers. "I figured let Steve and Marcus deal with the kids and their parents, just point out that bullying and assaulting someone isn't acceptable under any circumstances. I'm not pressing charges. It's up to the school to deal out whatever punishment it sees fit. And if Mr. Tovey could call a whole school assembly, I figured you, Jem, Ben when he gets back, and I could do an anti-bullying talk."

Nate laughed. "I love it."

Mr. Tovey nodded. "I'll organize that now. I really am very sorry. I'll make sure all the lunchtime controllers and teaching and support staff sit in on it as well."

Dane smiled for the first time. "Thank you."

❧

Amy walked slowly out to the police car. Her heart pounded. She struggled for every breath she took, and her stomach twisted to the point of throwing up, even though she hadn't eaten for hours.

Dane's a cop? How could I have not known? The signs were there, if only I'd worked it out. Why didn't he tell me?

The uniformed officer, whose name she didn't remember, opened the door. Her throat closed on her, making breathing now nigh on impossible. Memories of the last time she was in the back of a police car assailed her. The car door thudded shut, and she jumped.

Vicky held her hand tightly as the car started.

Amy closed her eyes. Why had Dane put her in this position? Of course he didn't know. He was just trying to do what he thought best for his daughter as she'd failed in her duty of care to her. She'd trusted the teachers to deal with it and they hadn't and now Dane was mad at her for not telling him. And rightly so. He should be mad at her.

The car stopped, and she opened her eyes. They were back at the house. The police officer let them out, and she managed a small smile. "Thank you."

"You're welcome."

Amy led Vicky up the path and unlocked the front door. As Vicky ran inside, Amy deactivated the burglar alarm and then hung up her coat. She sucked in a deep breath and followed Vicky into the kitchen.

Vicky looked at her.

"Well, now you have the afternoon off, what shall we do?"

Vicky shrugged.

"You know you're not in trouble, right?" Amy got down next to her. "Daddy wasn't cross with you. He jumped over the school fence to get to you and save you. So did Uncle Nate."

Vicky raised an eyebrow and moved her hands slowly. Was she using sign language? The gestures were slow to be sure, but very deliberate.

"Seriously, he did. You should have seen him. It was just like on those TV shows about the police, and he did it just to get to you. I got the teachers out there, but your dad had sorted it when we got there."

Vicky moved her hands again. It had to be sign

language. She knew Dane and Jodie used it at times and with Nate's wife being deaf, it made sense they all knew it.

"I wish I could understand you. But I sat outside the school watching the playground to make sure you were safe."

Vicky shook her head.

"I know you weren't, sweetie, but you are now. Daddy and I will make sure of it."

Vicky hugged her.

Amy hugged her back. "Now I don't know about you, but I'm thirsty. So, why don't we have a drink before we make the pudding? Would you like juice or milk?" The doorbell rang. "Tell you what, I'll see who that is, while you decide what to drink." She got up and headed into the hall. She opened the door.

Nate's car was parked on the drive.

Adeline stood there, her dog Ben at her heels. She looked worried. "Hi. Nate rang and told me what happened. He asked if I'd come over and make sure you and Vicky are all right."

"Come in. We're both a bit shaken." She shut the front door. She had to remember to face Adeline whenever she spoke so Adeline could read her lips. Vicky ran into the hall and got down next to Ben, petting him.

Amy looked at her, then back at Adeline. "Wait a minute. Nate *rang* you? How does that work?"

Adeline grinned. "I have special software on my phone. He speaks, I get a text message, and he hears my reply."

"Very clever. Would you like some tea?"

"Thank you. Tea would be good." She hung up her coat.

"I want to ask you something, only it may make me sound like an idiot. Vicky was moving her hands in reply when I spoke to her just now. Very deliberately. I wondered if she was using sign language, but I don't know it so didn't understand any of what she said."

Adeline watched Vicky. "Sweetheart?"

Vicky shrugged.

Amy knelt beside her. "It's OK, sweetie. I just thought if you were using sign language like Daddy and Jodie do sometimes, then maybe I could learn it too and we could communicate a little better. We don't have to."

Vicky moved her hands.

Amy wondered about the huge grin that crossed the blonde woman's face. "Well?"

Adeline nodded. "It's sign. She says thank you for helping her."

Amy looked back at Vicky. "You're welcome, sweetie. I'm sorry I wasn't fast enough."

Vicky hugged her.

Amy blinked hard and glanced at Adeline who was crying. "Are you OK?"

"That's the first thing she's 'said' since Jasmine died," Adeline said. "We should text Dane."

Vicky shook her head, signing slowly.

Amy frowned. "What did she say?"

"She said she wants to surprise him when he comes home."

"She'll certainly do that." Amy smiled. "Can you teach me? At least the basics so I can understand her a little."

Adeline nodded. "Sure. I can come over each day and teach you if you like."

"I'd like that a lot. Thank you."

Vicky pointed to the kitchen and tugged Amy's hand.

She grinned. "I don't need a translation for that. We have to learn over making the pudding. I haven't forgotten."

8

Dane stood with Nate in the takeaway waiting for their order. The smell of the food cooking made his stomach growl. But then he'd ended up working through lunch. Again. "At least the guv wasn't mad this time," he said wryly. "I'm actually surprised she didn't blow her top."

Nate looked at him. "She's got kids. Any parent would have reacted the same way. Besides, you didn't lose it and you didn't handle those bullies yourself. Plus you turned the whole thing into a positive. Hopefully the kids will have learnt, the parents will take on board what was said in the letters that went home, and the staff will be a little more vigilant in the playground."

"If not then I look at other primary schools in the area and move her." Dane sucked in what he hoped was a deep calming breath. "I just hope she's all right."

"Vicky will be fine. Or did you mean Amy?"

"I don't know what you mean." Although he had to admit Amy had looked awful today. And when he suggested going home in the patrol car, he honestly thought she was going to pass out. Completely freaked wasn't a strong enough description. If she could have run away, she probably would have.

Nate rolled his eyes. "I've seen the way you look at her. Your eyes light up, your skin flushes, your breathing increases."

"It does not." Dane knew his skin was flushing again now, and he was decidedly hot under the collar. He undid his coat.

Nate grinned. "That proves my point. And it's about time."

"She's my children's nanny."

"She's a woman."

"I had noticed." Dane loosened his tie. "Is it me or is it hot in here?"

"And you like her." Nate wasn't going to let this go.

Dane sighed. "It doesn't matter if I do. She's the nanny. I'm her employer."

Nate elbowed him. "Hey, I fell for a witness during an active murder investigation. At least you're falling for someone who's not being hunted by a serial killer or worse. And you're not likely to get a dressing down from the guv *and* MI5 as a result."

"I shouldn't fall for her at all." He pulled out his wallet to pay for the food. "I hardly know her, but she lights up a room simply by walking into it. It's nice to have someone to talk to in the evenings. And to cook for, though to be honest, she seems to have taken over the cooking herself, even though it's not part of her duties." He picked up the bags of food. "Thank you."

Nate took some of the bags. "Will we eat this much?"

"You'll be surprised." He opened the door.

"You should take Amy out somewhere."

"Huh?" He looked at Nate in confusion. *Where did that come from?* "I can't do that."

"Sure you can. It's easy." They reached the car. He waited while Dane unlocked it. "You look at her, and say 'Amy, will you come to the movies, or the theatre, or have dinner with me?' She'll say 'what about the kids?' You say 'Nate's babysitting'. She then smiles, blushes, looks extremely cute and says 'yeah, thank you, I'd like that.'"

"Really?"

Nate laughed and got in the car, arranging the bags by his feet. "Well, words to that effect, yeah."

"You, babysit?" Dane scrunched up his nose, leaning on the passenger door. "You haven't offered to do that, ever."

"Until now, you've refused to let anyone other than your parents near the girls, and that was simply for school runs if you didn't do them yourself. I was a single parent for years, remember? And Jas babysat for me so I could attend elders meetings and so on. It's about time you got out and started doing things again."

Dane shook his head and got in the car. He started the engine. Even if he did ask, she probably wouldn't say yes. Would he spoil things between them if he did take her out? He had no idea how she felt about him. Nate said it was obvious, but then it had been a long time since he'd needed to work out how a woman felt or what she was thinking.

This didn't have to be a date, he decided. He could phrase it as a chance to talk to her away from the house and the kids. That's if she wanted to go anywhere with him in the first place, or if she wanted anything to do with him now. Did she think he'd fire her for not telling him her suspicions about Vicky? Yes, he'd been angry initially, but she'd done something about it, rather than just letting things go until later.

His mind moved onto a different track. Maybe her problem was his job. What did she have against cops?

That had thrown her more than anything. That was when the obvious panic had set in. She'd been angry she saw Vicky crying and then being hurt. That much was evident from the way she'd gone into the school, armed with photographic evidence with only her concerns to go on.

He knew that both her parents were dead—Jodie had told him that. He wondered why Amy hadn't mentioned it. Were they cops? Had they died in the line of duty? That would account for her fear. Or perhaps they'd died some other way and her final memory of them was a police car arriving and a uniformed officer at the door.

Either way he needed to talk to her and sort things out. As he pulled onto the drive beside Nate's car, the house looked warm and welcoming with lights blazing from every window.

Nate picked up the bags of food and followed him to the front door.

It opened as they reached it, Dane's key not even making the keyhole. Loud music blasted past him from the study.

Jodie's face lit up. "Hi, Dad, did you bring the food? I'm starving."

Dane held out his empty hands. "No. What food? Was I meant to bring food with me?"

"Daaaaddddd. You said we could have fish and chips…" Jodie moaned. "We're starving. Amy hasn't cooked anything. Other than the stickiest, yummiest looking chocolate pudding you've ever seen. But we're not even allowed to touch it until after dinner."

Nate laughed, holding up the bags. "It's a good job I've got the dinner then, isn't it?"

"Then you can come in. Dad can't." Jodie grinned.

"Oh, I see how it is," Dane grumbled, hanging up his coat. "Where's Vicky? Is she OK?"

"She's in the kitchen with Amy and Auntie Adeline. Vianne and I are doing homework in the study."

Dane tilted his head, raising an eyebrow. "Homework, really? Sounds like a whole lot of studying being done in there."

Jodie rolled her eyes. "It's music homework. Mr. Weston said we have to listen to stuff, full blast and write down how it makes us feel."

Nate shook his head. "Really?"

"Yeah, really."

"And how does it make you feel?" Dane asked.

"Deaf," Jodie grinned. "Other than that, the jury is still out." She headed back to the study. "Dinner's here, Vianne," she yelled.

Dane headed into the kitchen, Nate behind him.

Amy nudged Vicky. "Daddy's home."

Vicky launched herself across the room at him, hugging him tightly.

He lifted her into his arms, kissing her cheek. "Hey, honey. How are you? Are you OK, now?"

She shrugged.

From the corner of his eye, he saw Adeline hug Nate and sign to him. Then he turned to Amy. "Was she OK when you got back here?"

"Yeah, just very quiet. Adeline and Ben came over just after we got in. We've kept her busy. She made the pudding extra chocolaty."

"And what about you?"

She glanced at her wrist. "I'm fine." She turned to get the plates out.

Dane paused. He hadn't meant her wrist, but he

wasn't going to push the issue now. He'd talk to her later, once the kids were in bed. He looked at Vicky. "I bet cooking was fun, huh?"

She nodded.

"And extra chocolate?"

She nodded again.

He sat down with her on his lap. "Well, Uncle Nate and I spoke to everyone at your school, while the uniformed officers spoke to the girls who hurt you. We told them that bullying and hitting other people aren't acceptable and won't be tolerated. It won't happen again."

She tilted her head at him.

"I promise. And Mr. Tovey said he'll keep a special eye out for the next few weeks."

Amy put the plates on the bench. "What happened to the girls involved?"

"They've been excluded for the rest of this week and the first week back after half term."

"Half term is next week, right?"

He nodded. "Yeah."

"Did they say why they picked on her?"

"I'll fill you in on all the details later."

"OK." Amy nodded and dropped her gaze.

He turned back to his daughter. "And it's almost the holiday. You get a whole week off school. Maybe there's something you'd like to do. Go riding or swimming or something."

Vicky tilted her head and moved her hands.

Dane jerked and straightened.

His heart skipped a beat, and his breath caught in his throat.

Was he imagining things?

Did she just—

No, surely he was seeing things. He so wanted her to talk to him, that it was like seeing an oasis in the middle of the desert.

He glanced over at Amy who just grinned at him. Nate and Adeline had similar expressions on their faces. He looked back at Vicky. "Honey?"

Vicky repeated the gestures slowly and deliberately.

Tears burned his eyes. She had "spoken" for the first time in months. His heart filled and overflowed.

He wasn't imagining things. She was speaking to him.

"Of course you can have a light party for Halloween," he said hugging her tightly. He closed his eyes, grateful for Nate's insistence they all learn sign when he and Adeline got engaged.

Prayers of thanks and praise filled him. He'd gotten his daughter back, or at least she was on the way back.

Thank You, God, she finally "spoke" to me.

He gradually opened his eyes, tears falling unhurriedly. "Who do you want to come?"

Vicky signed slowly.

Dane smiled through the tears. "That sounds great. Vianne and Lara can come. Anyone else?"

She shook her head.

"What's a light party?" Amy asked, putting the plates of fish and chips on the table for the girls.

"The opposite of a Halloween party," Vianne said. "It means we don't miss out as we're not allowed to go trick or treating because it's 'evil.'" She put speech marks around the word evil.

Nate looked at her. "You know very well why you're not allowed to go," he said sharply. "But you'll enjoy it the same as always." He turned to the table, taking the lids off the rest of the food containers. "You should ask Pastor Jack and Cassie as well. We could have dinner while the kids play."

Dane nodded. "That's a good idea."

Vicky tugged at his sleeve and signed to him.

He nodded. "You ask her."

She rolled her eyes and signed some more.

"Oh, yeah, good point. OK. Amy, Vicky wonders if you can make that special cake you told her about for the party. She says you can't read her signs well enough for her to ask you herself."

Amy laughed. "I can't read much at all, as I've only had the one lesson. But, yes, I can make the cake."

Dane looked at Vicky. "A special cake, huh?" He read her signs and raised an eyebrow before looking over at Amy. "A *fairy castle*?"

Amy grinned. "With turrets, drawbridges, castellations, you know, the whole works." She lowered her voice and used a stage whisper. "And it comes with fairies too."

"How on earth do you make one of those?"

Jodie rolled her eyes. "She'll wave her fairy wand, Dad. Don't you know anything?" She sat at the table with Vianne, picking up a glass of soda and sipping it.

Dane laughed. "Of course she will."

Amy sat down as the others did. She looked at Dane. "Don't let it get cold."

Nate grinned and signed over at him. "See, she nags like a wife. Best ask her out pronto."

"You're lucky I like you," Dane signed back. Then he reverted to audible speech. "Nate, will you say grace and we can start? Don't want this getting cold."

Nate nodded and said grace.

Vicky tugged his sleeve.

"Yes, honey."

She signed slowly.

Tears ran down his face, and he signed back. "I love you, too. So very, very much."

❧

He came back downstairs, having settled the girls into bed. Making two cups of cocoa, he took them through to the lounge and handed one to Amy.

"Thank you." She wrapped her hands around the mug. "I'm really sorry I didn't tell you about the photos or my suspicions about the bullying."

"You should have, but I can understand how it happened," he said, sitting down in his usual chair.

"I will next time."

"As far as this bullying goes, there won't be a next time," he said firmly. "I will make sure of that."

"You never did tell me why they did it."

"Because she won't speak to them. It marked her out as different, weird, and you know how much kids hate that." He took a long drink of the cocoa, the scent and warmth filling him, relaxing him as well.

Amy sipped from her cup. "But she's signing now. She'll get there. I still can't believe you scaled the fence like that. Do you do that a lot in your line of work?"

He glanced up. "It does happen occasionally." He sucked in a deep breath. "Do you have something against police officers?"

"No." She spoke far too quickly for his liking.

"It's just you seemed spooked when you found out earlier."

She studied her mug for a long time before

answering. "It's nothing," she finally said quietly. "I just didn't realize you were a cop. You hadn't said what you did for a job."

"It hadn't come up. Are you sure it's not a problem?"

Again, she paused, not looking at him. "No, it's not a problem."

"OK."

He glanced at her then down at his cup. For a moment, he wondered if Nate was wrong and now was *not* the time to ask her. Because he didn't believe her when she said she didn't have a problem with cops. If he didn't know better, he'd say she was scared of them and there had to be a reason for that. But at the same time, she was still here. Alone, with him. That must mean something. Didn't it? Oh, what did he have to lose?

"Amy?"

She looked up. "For the record, I know not all cops are the same. You and Nate have changed my mind about that."

He smiled. "Good."

"Sorry. I interrupted you. What were you going to say?"

"I was wondering if you'd have dinner with me tomorrow night."

"We have dinner every night."

"I know, but I mean *dinner*. Just you and me, a restaurant somewhere, and no kids. Nate has offered to babysit."

She held his gaze, a delightful blush slowly spreading from her cheeks up to her hairline. For a moment indecision flickered in her eyes, then she smiled. "I'd like that. Thank you."

9

Dane pushed Amy's chair in and then sat opposite her. "This seems intensely wicked," he said. "The girls will never forgive us."

Amy grinned. "Then we don't tell them. I mean it's a pizza place not a burger joint, so it's not a huge sin, just a tiny one."

Dane patted his stomach. "Tell my waistline that in the morning. I won't be able to jump over any more fences. Or chase bad guys."

She rolled her eyes. "Oh, well now, we can't have that."

"Nate can do it. He gets plenty of practice running around after Vianne and Ben."

Amy picked up the menu. "And you don't, running after the girls."

He winked. "That's what I pay you for."

"True." She glanced up at the waiter. "I think I'll have the meat feast. And a glass of lemonade with lots of ice and lemon, please."

Dane chuckled. "You don't strike me as the meat feast type. I'll have the barbeque chicken with peppers and extra chili, with a glass of lemonade, no ice. Can we have a side of onion rings and potato wedges, please?"

The waiter took the menus and headed back to the kitchen.

Amy looked down at her hands, twisting the

necklace around her fingers.

Dane looked at her. "Penny for them."

"Just thinking. Dad liked chili. The hotter and spicier the food was, the better. I'd have to send out bottles of the sauces when he was Det."

Dane tilted his head. "Det?"

"Detached, umm, a short overseas tour. Dad was in the RAF for years."

"Ah. What my US friend would call TDY."

She frowned. "Maybe. Anyway, he'd be gone for months at a time. But for a while Mum was around and it was hard, but bearable."

"What happened to your mum?" he asked as the drinks arrived.

Amy picked up her glass, her hands trembling. "I was ten when she died. That's why..."

"Why you took the job, and are so good with the girls," he said. "Because you know exactly how they feel."

Amy nodded. She blinked hard. "After Mum died, I stayed on base with Dad, went wherever he was posted. Depending on where it was, of course. When he got posted to a war zone, I had to stay behind."

"Was that often?"

"Too often. They married young. Mum was only thirty-one when she died. Dad was forty-two. He was killed by an IED while I was at university."

"I'm sorry."

The pizza arrived, and they concentrated on serving themselves for a moment. Amy pulled a piece of pepperoni off the top of her slice. "It was really hard. If it hadn't been for Rosalie and Ray, I don't know what I would have done."

"Are they friends of yours?"

"Best friends. Rosalie and I met on our first day at St. Andrews, studied the same course, flat shared and did everything together. Ray Malone was the assistant pastor at the church we went to while we were at university. He ended up marrying Rosalie just after our final exams finished, and when he got his first pastorate, as I had no ties, I went with them. They moved into the manse and I rented a small place not far from them. They just had their first baby—Sara. This is the first time in years we've been separated."

"Sounds like you miss them."

"Yeah, I do. Rosalie is more like a sister than a friend. She always knew how I felt simply by the way I said hello. She makes a fantastic pastor's wife. Ray is the most amazing preacher and I'm not just saying that. He has a real gift for exposition and Bible-based teaching. Very much like your Pastor Jack, actually. And the baby is so cute. And so tiny. She'll be six weeks old now, or thereabouts."

Grief emanated from her, as she picked at her food. He wished he hadn't asked, but she spoke of them with such love. What had happened to make her leave?

Dane picked up another slice from his plate. "I shouldn't have asked. I'm sorry."

"It's fine. We just spent so much time together, told each other everything. We didn't have any secrets from each other. It was the kind of friendship many people can only dream about. After Dad died, she was all I had. Losing her is like losing part of me. I'm alone now."

Had her friend died? She hadn't said as much, but reading between the lines, if she missed her that much and she wasn't dead, why not simply pick up the phone. Had they parted on bad terms?

Dane watched her. "You should call them."

"I don't think so." She pulled at the pizza. "Sometimes stuff happens that you can't control, turning everything on its head, and once it does, you find you can't go back no matter how much you want to."

"But if you've been such good friends for years, then surely nothing is too great to overcome. And I'm sure a pastor and his wife would be more forgiving than most."

She shrugged. "Not this time."

He took a bite of his pizza. He'd have to look up Pastor Ray Malone online, and contact him. Maybe he could help Amy the way she was helping him, by giving her back the only family she had.

Amy took a deep breath. "Have you gone to Headley Baptist long?"

He swallowed and picked up an onion ring. "Yes, I've been going there for a long time, actually for more years than I'm going to admit. I got married there, the kids were dedicated there."

She swirled the liquid in her glass. "It must be nice, to be so settled and to actually belong somewhere. I never really had anywhere to lay my hat and call home."

"Oh?"

"Military brat, remember. I was never in the same place for more than three years."

"It must've been hard."

"Yeah…" She looked down at her glass, her eyes clouded. "I thought I'd finally found it with Rosalie and Ray," she whispered. "But it wasn't to be."

Dane cleared his throat. "Anyway, the two weeks

are up and I was wondering..."

She glanced at Dane, worry mixing with the fear and grief on her face. Her fingers white against the clear fizzy liquid in her glass. "Yeah?"

"The girls love having you around. You do a great job with them. You got Vicky to communicate."

"Well, not exactly."

"Amy, don't underestimate what you did. Thanks to you, she's communicating with more than just a nod or a shake for the first time since her mum died. Signing is a huge step forward. I can't thank you enough for that. So, if you want to stay on, if you can put up with Jodie's tantrums, we'd like it. I'd like it."

Her eyes lit up. "Thank you. So would I. I'll belong..." She broke off.

"Go on." He reached across, laying a hand over hers, trying to ignore the warmth and slight jolt that shot up his arm straight to his heart and then curled around his stomach.

"Belong somewhere, even if only for a little while."

He squeezed her hand. "For as long as you want," he told her. "I think you need us as much as we need you. God placed you here for a reason, Amy. Not just to help Vicky."

She looked at him. "I don't know about that."

"He'll show us in His own good time," Dane assured her. "Now, are you going to help me with these onion rings? Because I really don't want to have to take a doggy bag home, no matter how much the girls would like cold pizza and onion rings for breakfast."

She reached out and took one. "So what about you? How long have you been a cop?"

"Ever since I left school. It was all I ever wanted to be. I went to Police College and trained and qualified. Worked my way up through uniform, then transferred to CID. Did general stuff for a couple of years, then transferred to the department I'm in now. I made sergeant about ten years ago and have been partnered with Nate for almost as long. I can't imagine doing anything else."

"Isn't it dangerous?"

He studied her. That must be the problem—his job was dangerous, but he didn't think of it like that. To him it was simply what he did. "Climbing fences and chasing bad guys?"

She nodded. "I mean, you hear of officers getting shot and killed. Or stabbed. Doesn't it worry you that you might go to work one day and not come home?"

He bit into an onion ring, chewing slowly. "A little." He waved the ring as he spoke. "But I could get hit by a car walking down the street tomorrow."

Amy visibly shuddered and closed her eyes for a moment. "Yeah, I guess so."

He frowned. "But, there's no point worrying about something I can't control. I just have to love my girls and do my job to the best of my ability. So, how about we change the subject and talk about something light-hearted and silly for a bit."

She looked at him. "Like what?"

"How about the time the girls got ahold of my shaving foam and decided to see how far it would go?" He grinned. "It went from the bathroom, across the landing, down the stairs..."

Amy stood with her hands on her hips in the bedroom doorway. Jodie lay curled up in bed, under the duvet. "You're going to be late, Jodie."

"Don't care."

Amy pulled the duvet down. "Get up."

Jodie shook her head. "No. Leave me alone." She yanked the duvet back up and vanished beneath it.

Amy sighed. "I will not leave you alone until you talk to me."

"Don't want to go to school."

"You have to go. It's the law."

"Well, that law stinks." Jodie's voice was muffled under the covers.

"Fine. You don't go to school. They arrest your dad and he goes to prison."

"That won't happen." Jodie stiffened under the duvet. "You're lying."

"No, I'm not. Now, do I have to ring your dad and get him to come back here? Which would get him into trouble with his boss as well?"

"No." She pushed down the duvet and shook her head vehemently. "You can't tell him. He'll freak if he finds out, and I'll be grounded for like the next six months at least."

"Then tell me why you don't want to go in. Maybe I can help, like I did with Vicky. Are you in trouble? Is someone picking on you, too?"

She nodded slightly. "I'm in trouble, yeah, but no one's picking on me."

Amy sat on the bed beside her. "So tell me what's wrong and I'll fix it, if I can."

"It's a long story, but if I go in, I need you to come in after school tonight to see one of my teachers."

"Why?"

"To get my phone back. He confiscated it."

Amy studied her. That explained why Jodie hadn't gone out to youth club the previous evening like she normally did—one of Dane's unbreakable rules was if Jodie went out after dark, she took her phone with her. "Who confiscated it?"

"My English teacher—Mr. Page. I was texting during a lesson. I had detention at break yesterday and have it again today at lunchtime. I have a letter you need to sign to say you know about it. He'll only give the phone back to a parent or caregiver. Dad said he put you in charge when he's not here and right now he's at work, so you're it."

"I can do that. What time do I have to be there?"

"Mr. Page said after school tonight."

"Then I'll meet you at the gate once I've picked up Vicky, but only if you get up now. Being late isn't going to make things any better. In fact I can guarantee you'll probably get more detentions out of it."

"OK."

Amy smiled in relief as Jodie sat up. "See, that wasn't so bad, was it?"

"You haven't met Mr. Page."

಄ೲ

That afternoon, Jodie led her through the hallway to the English department and knocked on the open office door. "Mr. Page?"

A tall, dark haired, bearded man looked up. "Come in, Jodie."

Amy looked at Vicky. "Sit here for a minute, sweetie."

Vicky nodded, sitting down on the chair in the

hallway and swinging her legs.

Amy followed Jodie into the office.

"I've come to get my phone back." Jodie's tone was sullen, and she shoved her hands into her pockets.

Mr. Page studied her. "I've come to get my phone back...what?"

Jodie huffed. "I've come to get my phone back...please." She paused. "Sir."

"I can only give it back to a parent, you know that."

"Dad's always working. This is Amy, our nanny."

Amy held out a hand. "Amy Stabler. Mr. Philips put me in charge of the girls while he's working. I hope I'll do in place of him."

"Liam Page, Jodie's English teacher and head of department." His grip was firm and his hands warm.

"It's nice to meet you. Although you look kind of familiar."

Jodie sighed. "Mr. Page goes to our church. He sits in the pew behind us with his wife. You'd have seen him on Sundays. Now can I *please* have my phone back?"

Mr. Page frowned at her. "What are the rules governing phones in school?"

She shuffled her feet. "No using them in class. They should be switched off at all times. In case of a parental emergency, they can get hold of us via the school office. Likewise the school office can contact our parents if we get injured or something else happens."

"So why did you have your phone out in my class?"

Jodie shrugged.

Mr. Page narrowed his eyes. "I won't ask you again, Jodie."

Amy nudged her. "Answer him."

"I was sending Fran a text."

"Fran sits next to you, doesn't she?"

"Yes, she does, but we're not allowed to talk or pass notes in class, and I had to tell her something really important. So I sent her a text instead."

"Texting isn't allowed any more than talking or passing notes. If it was that important, then you address your comment to the entire class by putting your hand up and asking permission to speak."

"It wasn't something the whole class needed to know."

"And it couldn't have waited until the end of the lesson?"

"No, sir, it couldn't have."

Mr. Page looked at her. "Then you not only got yourself in trouble, but Fran as well. I will be sending a letter to her mother tomorrow morning."

"But how did you know I was using the phone? It was on silent and you were writing on the board."

"I wasn't born yesterday," he told her. "And the glass bookcase next to the board means I effectively do have eyes in the back of my head."

"Oh."

Mr. Page unlocked the desk drawer, opened it, and pulled out the phone. "I don't want to see your phone again. If I do, it will be confiscated for a week, not just for twenty-four hours. You'll also get a week of detention and your club privileges revoked for the rest of term. And I will be giving the phone back to your father rather than your nanny, is that understood?"

Jodie snatched the phone, putting it into her pocket. "'K."

Amy glared at her. "Answer Mr. Page properly."

"Yes, sir. I understand perfectly," Jodie muttered.

Amy frowned and hardened her voice. "Answer him properly without the attitude, young lady. Otherwise a week of detention, no clubs, and a confiscated phone will be the least of your worries."

Jodie looked at her, panic flickering in her eyes. "You can't tell Dad. He'll blow his top if he finds out."

"I won't need to tell him. You know you're not allowed to leave the house after dark without your phone. You want to explain to your dad why you're staying in every night for a whole week when you're not grounded?"

"No," she whispered. She slowly looked back at her teacher. "I'm sorry, sir. It won't happen again."

Mr. Page nodded. "Good. Thank you. Jodie, can you wait outside a moment, while I speak to Miss Stabler, please?"

"'K." She headed outside and shut the door.

"Please, have a seat."

"Thank you, Mr. Page."

"It's Liam. I've been meaning to say hello the past couple of Sundays. It's nice to finally get the chance."

"I'm just sorry it's like this. Jodie isn't the happiest of children at the best of times."

Liam nodded. "I'm worried about her, to be honest. Her work has really suffered the past three or four months and her grades are well down on what they were. She was a grade A student, even after her mother died, but now..." He pulled out a file and handed Amy a sheet of paper. "She's struggling to make a D. She hasn't handed in any homework for weeks, either. This is her last piece of creative writing. After I read it, I was going to ask Dane to come in, but as you're here, maybe you could shed some light on it instead. What she's put is disturbing to put it mildly. Not to mention worrying. For someone her age to be so distraught that she thinks the only way out is dying, isn't something you come across every day. I honestly think there is more to it than a simple class writing task."

Amy read it. "It's not a great surprise," she said quietly. "Jodie's always drawing pictures that contain gravestones with her initials on them. I'll talk to her."

"If there is anything I can do to help, let me know. We do have a counselor at the school, and if Dane thinks it's warranted I can refer her."

"I will." She stood up and gave him the papers back. "Thank you." She headed outside to where the girls sat. "OK, let's go home and get tea on for your dad."

"What did he want?"

"He's worried about your grades and lack of homework."

"Yeah, well, English is boring."

"Unfortunately, it's a necessary evil. You need it."

"I want to be an architect."

"You still need English. How else are you going to read the plans? Or submit a planning proposal or a patent?"

"Oh."

Amy nodded slowly. "But, if you'd like, I'll help you with it. Get you back on track."

"You will?" Jodie looked hopeful.

"However, you have to promise me you'll try. Otherwise, Mr. Page is going to have to talk to your dad."

"OK. I'll try."

"Cool. So how much homework is overdue?"

Jodie shrugged and looked around. "About six weeks' worth so six pieces."

Amy sighed. "So we start tonight and tackle one piece a night. How does that sound?"

Jodie rolled her eyes. "Like a heck of a lot of work."

Amy winked. "Also might shock Mr. Page. Not to mention it'll give him a whole lot of extra marking to do."

"Sounds good to me."

10

The next morning Amy came home from the school run to find Jodie's coat and bag still in the hall. She sighed and shut the front door and hung up her coat. Then she took the stairs, two at a time, as noisily as she could. So much for the promises Jodie had made the previous day, as they'd completed the first piece of homework which Jodie had planned on handing in that day.

Amy pushed open Jodie's bedroom door, not bothering to knock.

Jodie lay curled up on the bed, sobbing. Huge, heartbreaking sobs that shook her whole body. Her hands gripped her stomach tightly. Maybe she wasn't skiving this time. She was sick.

Amy sat on the bed next to her. "What's wrong, sweetie?"

"Dying..." Jodie choked out between sobs.

Amy gently rubbed her back, trying to comfort her. "I'm sure you're not. What's wrong?"

"Am."

"Jodie, talk to me. Something's been wrong for a while and all the gravestones you've drawn tell me it's something huge and really bothering you."

"I'm dying."

"Sweetie, you're not dying. But if you're sick, then I can take you to a doctor."

"No..." Fear flashed in Jodie's face.

"Then tell me what's wrong. Maybe there's something I can do to help."

"My stomach hurts," she whispered. "Hurts a lot." She reached under the bed and handed over a bag full of bloodied clothing. "I can't stop it."

Amy looked at her, the penny dropping. "Oh, Jodie." She put the bag down and hugged her tightly. "How long, sweetie?"

"Three months. I'm running out of clothes cos I throw them away, but it doesn't matter."

"I promise you, you're not dying. This is perfectly normal. It means you're a woman now and not a little girl anymore. I'll show you what to do as I have some stuff in my room. Then, after I've rung the school and told them you won't be in today, we'll make some cocoa and have a woman-to-woman chat. After that, we'll go to the chemist, and I'll get you everything you'll need. I can wash all this, and we'll buy you new things, too. But you're *not* dying."

Relief sparked in her eyes. "Really?"

"Really." Amy hugged her.

Ten minutes later, they sat in the kitchen, steaming cups of cocoa and marshmallows in front of them. Comfort food, especially designed for that time of the month.

Horror crossed Jodie's face. "At least five days, every month, for years? Why didn't anyone tell me?"

"Didn't the school have lessons?"

Jodie wrinkled her nose. "Well, only about yucky stuff and boys."

"And I guess your dad didn't know how to talk to you about this."

"Dad knows about this stuff? But it doesn't affect him at all."

"Yeah, he knows. It's just not something men like to talk about. But yeah, all men know about this, especially the married ones."

"So I'm not dying?"

Amy shook her head. "Nope, you're not dying. Not for a long time yet. So promise me, no more gravestones."

"I promise." Jodie tilted her head. "Although, didn't we already have that conversation?"

Amy rolled her eyes. "Ack, don't you get cheeky with me, madam. And that was homework, not gravestones."

"Same thing." Jodie laughed.

Amy grinned. "And in future, don't hide the clothes under the bed. Just rinse them in cold water and put them straight in the washing machine. I do washing almost every day anyway." She hugged her. "And if you need the sheets changed, let me know."

Jodie hugged her back. "Thank you, Amy."

"You're welcome, sweetie."

ॐ∘ॐ

Each day over the half-term break, Amy took the girls out for at least part of the day. They went swimming, horseback riding, to the park or into town. She'd finally gotten them to try on all their clothes and worked out what fitted and what didn't. What didn't fit was bagged up and put in the clothing bin in the recycling center.

She took the girls shopping, which wasn't the nightmare Dane said it would be. Vicky and Jodie even seemed to enjoy being given virtual free rein over their new clothes. Amy had to overrule a few of Jodie's choices, but on the whole both girls had good taste.

The difference in Jodie was marked. Now she knew she wasn't dying, she turned out to have a wicked sense of humor and would often offer to help do things without being asked. It was just a shame her father was too busy at work to notice.

Friday, the day of the light party, came all too quickly. As Nate and Adeline were at the hospital, Vianne was spending the entire day with Jodie and Vicky. Not that she saw them much, or that one more child really made that much difference to the chaos in the house.

The girls had shut themselves in the study making pictures and decorations for the dining room and the lounge. Music played at full volume from behind the closed door.

Amy had spent the morning assembling and icing the cake, before giving the girls lunch. The afternoon passed rapidly, as she busied herself with the rest of the food preparation for the evening. Dane had put a no trick-or-treating notice on the front door, which he assured her wouldn't result in the house getting egged.

Finally, the girls appeared with an arm full of bunting and pictures. She handed over enough tape and blu-tac to last a lifetime and set them to decorating the rooms as they saw fit, while she laid out the food on the dining table, taking care to make sure it was all covered with foil or cake covers to keep it fresh.

The phone rang. "Jodie, can you answer that, please?"

She looked at the table. She was missing something. But what?

Vicky tugged at her arm and signed to her.

"Of course. The cake. How could I forget?"

Vicky signed slowly enough for her to follow.

Amy mimed shock. "I am not old, you horror."

Vicky laughed and nodded.

She shook her head, laughing and went back to the kitchen, returning with the fairy castle cake. She placed it on the center of the table.

Vicky's eyes widened as she saw it.

Amy was pleased with how it had turned out. This time she'd added a moat and green coconut fields around it and taken several photos as she built it. The windows were wafer biscuits, coconut ice, and small colored sweets. The turrets were Swiss rolls topped with ice cream cones, the main body of the cake a Madeira sponge. The whole thing was covered in a delicious baby pink butter icing and sugar crystals. No doubt Dane would tut and complain about sugar overload, but it wasn't as if she did this every day of the week.

Jodie came in with the phone. "It's for you."

"Me? Is it your dad?"

"No. Some man, asked for you by name."

"Oh." The blood in her veins turned to ice, and she fought the desire to close her eyes. Whoever could it be? No one knew she was here. She wasn't on the electoral register and all her ID was fake. "Did he say who he was?"

"Nope. I'm figuring someone from church or something."

She took the phone. Perhaps Jodie was right. A nice simple explanation. "Hello?"

Silence. A long silence. Was that breathing? Surely the calls weren't going to start up again. She hung up and tugged down her red jumper.

She wandered across to the window to close the

curtains. A car pulled up and parked opposite. A tall figure dressed as the grim reaper got out and leaned against the car, staring at her. The door of the house across the road opened and a woman dressed as a cat stood outlined against the light, complete with ears and a long tail. There must be a party.

The phone rang again almost immediately. "Hello?"

Heavy breathing echoed in her ear. Then a deep husky voice, "Red suits you."

Amy screamed, dropping the phone, and pulling the curtains so fast, the pole came down narrowly missing her. It hit a vase, sending it smashing to the floor, glass spraying everywhere almost in slow motion.

She dropped to her knees amongst the broken glass shards. She struggled for breath, tears running down her face as panic flooded her.

He found me. How? I've been so careful.

11

Dane raced through the dark streets, driving as fast as he legally could. What could have happened? Jodie's phone message was garbled to say the least, panic spilling into her voice. Something about Amy crying and being far too upset to even move off the floor. The curtains were broken and a vase, and there was blood, too. He'd told Jodie to ring Pastor Jack and get him and Cassie to come over early and that he'd be home as soon as he could. He'd texted Nate, asking him to go straight to his place when he and Adeline left the hospital.

Dane swung onto the drive, relieved to see Pastor Jack's car parked there. Lights shone from all the windows. Pastor Jack stood in the lounge window, sweater sleeves pulled up to his elbows as he held something above his head. It looked as if he were fixing the curtains. Nodding a greeting to him, Dane ran up the path, pulling out his keys.

The door opened as he got to it. Pastor Jack stood there. "Hi."

"Pastor, thanks for coming. Where is she? Is she OK? What about the girls? Are they all right?"

"Amy's in the lounge with Cassie. The girls are fine. Jodie has them all decorating biscuits in the kitchen. I'm keeping half an eye on them and fixing your curtain pole, which is back up on the wall, now. Just need to rehang the curtains. I also re-bandaged

Amy's wrist. She cut it again on the broken glass from the vase. Jodie's got a good head on those shoulders. When we got here, she'd wrapped a towel around Amy's wrist and had gotten Vianne in the kitchen keeping Vicky occupied. They were singing in sign language."

"Thank you." Dane stripped off his coat. "Did she say what happened? Jodie's call didn't make much sense."

"Amy hasn't said anything. She's really too upset to do anything other than sit there, right now. I'll be in the kitchen if you need anything—let you talk to Amy alone."

Dane nodded and headed into the lounge.

Cassie got up. "I'll go help Jack with the girls."

"Thanks." He moved over to Amy and sat on the floor beside her. "Amy?"

She turned, almost throwing herself into his arms and clinging to him tightly, the same way Vicky did.

Taken aback, he held her fast as she sobbed. He didn't move, other than to comfort her, knowing that right now she needed his physical presence more than anything he could say. It had been a long time since he'd held a woman in his arms, yet his body stirred. He shook himself. Now wasn't the time for his long dormant emotions to wake. She needed him focused. But what could possibly have upset her so? Because something had scared her. And if that some*thing* turned out to be a some*one*, they weren't going to get away with it.

Finally the tears subsided, and the shaking stopped.

He reached into his pocket and gave her his hanky. "Here. What happened? Jodie was really worried. She said a man rang and you got really upset."

"Sorry," she managed, wiping her eyes.

"Don't be sorry. Has something happened to your friend? Did her husband call?"

"No. It wasn't Ray who rang."

"Do you know who it was?"

She shook her head slowly.

Dane frowned, puzzled. He'd been sure Jodie said the caller asked for Amy by name. Maybe he'd misheard her, but he had to make sure. "Jodie said he asked for you by name."

"I don't know him." She waved her hands. "Just an 'unpleasant' call."

"What did he say?" Dane's copper's instincts came on full alert. He knew all too well what those calls usually consisted of. He kept close hold of her, realizing his heart was beating in perfect time with hers.

"Heavy breathing. Told me I looked good in red," she whispered.

He closed his eyes, hiding his automatic reaction and swallowed down the surge of rage. "I'll get a trace put on the line in case he calls again."

"Please, don't. Just change the number."

He grimaced. "And if he does this to someone else?"

"Please, change the number."

"I can't just drop this." Every ounce of copper's blood in him told him what he had to do.

"Yes, you can. What if it's Jodie next time?" She looked up at him, her normally pale face red and blotchy. "Please, Dane, I beg you, just change the number."

Jodie stuck her head around the door. "I was thinking. Perhaps it's James."

Dane looked at her. "Who's James?"

"He's this really creepy nerd from my science class. He's also in my form. Ginger hair, freckles, glasses. He keeps going on and on about Amy and how she's hot." Jodie scrunched up her nose. "Not that you're not pretty, Amy, but you're old enough to be his mother. That's just ewwww. He must have gotten the landline number from my phone when he borrowed it to play a game a couple of days ago."

Dane raised an eyebrow. "James who?"

"He's just a numpty. He'll get over it."

"Jodie? Where did you get to?" Pastor Jack's voice echoed from the kitchen.

"Coming…" Jodie vanished again.

"See," Amy whispered. "Please, just change the number."

"OK." And he'd go ex-directory as well. And block the number so no one could find it by dialing 1-4-7-1.

"Thank you."

He hugged her. With all the cult activity going on up at Maranatha Farm, was it possible it was happening here in town as well? "Do you want me to cancel tonight?"

"No. The girls are looking forward to it. They've spent all day on the decorations." She glanced around. "Where are they?"

"Pastor Jack's had them busy in the kitchen icing biscuits. That's when he wasn't fixing your wrist and putting the curtain pole back up."

"I broke it. I'm sorry."

"Stop apologizing."

"OK. Pastor Jack is a man of many talents. God certainly blessed the church when He sent him as pastor."

Dane smiled. "That He did."

Amy took a deep breath. "I probably look a sight."

Dane took in her blotchy, swollen face and shook his head. "You're fine."

"Liar."

He paused, then nodded. "Not a very good one, I'm afraid." He rubbed the pad of his thumb over her lips. What would it be like to kiss her? His eyes searched hers. "Just as long as you're all right."

Amy held his gaze. She moved closer, her lips now a fraction away from his. "I think so."

He moved closer, his nose brushing against hers. "Amy..." He kissed her gently, his hand sliding around her neck, catching her earlobe.

She shuddered as she wrapped her arms around him, kissing him back.

He pulled her close, shutting his eyes as he kissed her again. She was responsive, her body soft against his. His nerve endings tingled and came alive, his heart pounding. Every fiber of his being reacted as if she were the first woman he'd ever kissed.

The door opened. Nate's voice shattered the moment. "Dane, is everything—" He broke off.

Dane pulled back, not letting go of Amy, who had gone a very attractive shade of bright red. "Everything's fine."

"I'll, uh, I'll be in the kitchen." Nate backed through the door, closing it behind him.

Dane grinned. "That is the first time I have ever seen him lost for words." He tilted his head, running his finger down Amy's jaw line and across her lips.

"Have I kissed you senseless?"

She nodded, not taking her gaze from his face.

"Can I do it again?"

She nodded.

Dane closed his eyes, losing himself in kissing her.

ॐ∘ॐ

Amy stood in the bathroom and rinsed her face. She looked a sight. She didn't want to believe it was Saunders. She'd been so careful. There was no contact with anyone from Filely. She had fake ID. A new phone and number. She was safe here. The time for living in fear and jumping at every shadow was over. The more she thought about it, the more she came to the conclusion that Jodie was right. It was probably that kid from the school. Perhaps he really did have a crush on her.

She allowed herself a slight smile. If need be, she'd get Dane to go do a talk on stalking to the kids in Jodie's year. Warn the boys against doing it, and tell the girls how to protect themselves and what to do if it actually happened.

Hoping the evidence of her so very public breakdown wasn't too obvious, Amy went into the kitchen. Despite her fears, she felt as if she were walking two feet off the ground. Dane's kisses had placed her very firmly on cloud nine, every part of her body singing.

Nate glanced over at her as she came into the room. "You OK?"

She nodded, hoping he hadn't said anything to the others about seeing them.

"Where's Dad?" Jodie asked.

"He's on the phone. I'm sorry about earlier. Didn't mean to panic or upset everyone."

Pastor Jack turned to her. "It's fine. We were about ready to come over anyway. Are you really OK?"

Amy nodded. "Yeah. Dane's changing the number so we don't get any more calls like that. He originally wanted to put a trace on the line, but then decided he didn't want Jodie answering the phone to some obscene caller."

"Good point," Nate said. "But a trace would have been better."

"There speaks a cop," Adeline said. "Sometimes that's not always the best way."

Vicky signed quickly.

Amy frowned, not sure what she'd said. "I didn't get all of that."

Adeline translated. "She wants to know if the number's being changed so you won't get upset anymore."

"Oh, right." Amy nodded. "Yes, that's why."

Nate grinned at Vicky. "So, where's this cake you've been raving on about?"

Her grin matched his as she signed a response.

"Yes, the huge fairy castle one."

"It's in the dining room on the table, ready for tea," Jodie said. "But Amy wants us to play games first."

Pastor Jack smiled. "That sounds like a lot of fun."

"We had to buy buns and apples," Jodie said. "And some fancy glass pens."

"I got some tea light holders for you to decorate," Amy explained. "You need special pens to write on the glass with, as ordinary ink just rubs off."

"Cool," the girls chorused.

Amy nodded. "First up are buns on a string."

Vianne looked puzzled. "What's that?"

"I have lots of buns tied onto pieces of string. And you have to eat them without using your hands."

The girls looked at each other. "That's not possible unless they are on the table."

"Nope. I hold the string."

"Show us." Jodie demanded.

Amy smirked, picking up a bun. "Then I need a volunteer."

Dane walked in, brushing his hands against his jeans. "OK, all done."

"Dad volunteers," Jodie said, with a huge grin.

He looked at her. "Dad volunteers for what?"

Amy chuckled. "Kneel down and put your hands behind your back."

Vicky signed rapidly at him.

Amy looked confused as everyone bar Dane laughed. He just rolled his eyes and poked his tongue out at his daughter.

Adeline looked at her. "She says he's under arrest."

Amy laughed. "Just kneel," she told him.

Dane grumbled, but knelt and put his hands behind his back. "No cuffs, Nate."

"I left them at home," Nate laughed. "But I can always go and get yours."

"Don't even think about it. Now what do I have to do?" Dane asked, his gaze never once leaving Amy's face.

She grinned and dangled the bun in front of him. "Eat this without using your hands."

"Easy," he said. He moved his face towards it, mouth open.

Amy laughed and moved the string.

"Hey, no fair," he complained as the girls shrieked with laughter.

"Perfectly fair," Amy said. "Wait until you demonstrate apple bobbing."

He shook his head. "Oh no, Nate can do that one. Just hold that string still."

Amy laughed, swinging it. "Nope."

Dane poked his tongue at her and tried again, missing, much to the delight of those watching. "This is impossible."

"Bet I can do it," Jodie said. She held one out to Nate. "Please."

Lara looked at Pastor Jack. "Do one for me, Daddy."

"And me," the others chorused, Vicky signing it.

❧❧

Clearing up after everyone had left, Amy picked up the glass pens and slid them back into the case. Decorating the tea light holders and making their own candles had definitely been a hit with the four girls, as well as the adults.

"That was a success," Dane said, coming back into the kitchen with the last of the dishes. "Thanks to you."

"Not just me. Everyone helped."

"Yes you. I'd never have thought of all the games and so on that you came up with. And that cake was amazing."

She shrugged. "The games were ones that we played as kids. We weren't allowed to go trick or treating. Not that it was as popular then as it is today."

Dane stacked the dishes in the dishwasher. "It's

coming from the US in a big way unfortunately. The kids think witches and ghosts are fun and don't see the danger in the whole thing."

"Yeah. Anyway, Grandad was a lay preacher, so Halloween was a banned thing. We went to their house and played games and had a candlelit tea instead."

"Yes, the candles at tea time were a touch of brilliance. Vicky's already asked if we can do it again. I told her maybe Sunday teatime, if she's good."

She wiped down the surfaces. "Sure."

"Everyone enjoyed themselves. Not just the children." He opened the cupboard and pulled down two mugs.

"Despite the fact I almost ruined the evening before it had even begun. Is the phone company going to charge you for the new number?"

"No, they aren't. Not for harassment calls. And you didn't ruin it." He turned to her, taking the cloth from her hands.

"I almost did. Freaking out like that over a stupid phone call. Jodie's probably right about it being that kid from school. I scared the girls…"

She shivered, hearing his voice hissing in her ear again. Seeing that grim reaper standing outside the house, staring at her, in his oh-so-apt costume, had scared her more than anything had in a while. What if Saunders did find her? What would she do?

What do I do, Lord, run again? I want so much to be safe and I thought I was safe here.

Dane's hand cradled her face. "Amy?"

She struggled to focus on him.

"It's OK."

"Never OK…" she whispered. Then his lips were on hers, and she kissed him, losing herself in the feelings his touch produced. His fingers wound through her hair, sending ripples of pleasure running through her. Time seemed to stand still as his hand pressed against the small of her back, almost burning her.

Dane pulled away. "I, uh, sorry."

"Don't apologize," she whispered.

"I should. Nate walked in on us earlier. It could have been one of the girls and I—"

Amy bit her lip. She'd crossed a line. Again. She took a step backwards and picked up the cloth. "Yeah, you're right."

"Amy, listen to me a minute. I'm not saying we can't do this at all. I'm saying we just need to be careful. Make sure we know this is what we want before the girls find out."

She caught her breath and nodded slowly. "What were you doing with the cups?"

"I was going to make cocoa." He turned to them. He took a deep breath and huffed it out. "Anyway, it's month end, and I ought to pay you. Did you want cash or a check? Or I can just transfer the money directly from my bank account to yours if you give me the details."

Amy thought fast. The one thing she hadn't got was a bank account in this name. She didn't want to risk her fake ID being found out. "Cash is fine, thank you."

"OK. I'll let you have it tomorrow. Speaking of paying things...did you say the gas man read the meter?"

"Yeah, ages ago. It was my second week here I think." She watched Dane frown. "Why?"

"I haven't had the bill yet. I might chase it up on

Monday. Make sure they sent it out."

"OK."

He put milk into the cups. "Jodie seems happier."

"Yeah. No more grave stones, and she's singing a lot now, too." She looked at him. "Although she is going to need a slightly bigger allowance than the one you're currently giving her."

"Oh?"

"Yeah. Like I said she's not a little girl anymore, but honestly, you could have warned her. Or at least asked Adeline to explain a few things to her if you were too embarrassed to do so yourself. She thought she was dying the last three months."

Dane looked puzzled, and paused as he put the mug into the microwave. "Why? She didn't seem sick. I'd have noticed if she was."

Amy groaned. "How long were you married? You've got kids, for goodness' sake, you know how things work. She got her period and had no idea what was happening. She was scared witless."

Color flushed his cheeks. "Oh."

"Yes, oh. Anyway, I've sorted her out. I explained how things work and took her to a chemist to show her what to get and bought her enough for now. So just give her a slightly bigger allowance to cover her expenses and she'll be fine. However, you didn't get this from me. She's too embarrassed about the whole thing still and didn't want me to tell you. But if she's shopping for herself she needs a raise in her allowance."

"I'll do that from the weekend. Thank you. It seems I'm in your debt again."

She smiled faintly. "Only until you pay me. Seriously, I'm just glad I could help."

Dane nodded, handing her a cup of steaming chocolate and putting his into the microwave to heat. "As it's Friday, the new number won't come into effect until Monday evening. So just don't answer the phone until then. If I need you, I'll text or ring your mobile. Unless I do what Nate has been suggesting for years and get an answerphone."

She shook her head. She was worrying for no reason. "I'm sure the new number will fix it."

"Hopefully, it will, yeah. I'm tempted to still get a trace put on the line, anyway."

"See if the new number works first, save bothering your work place with this." She looked at her cup, inhaling the sweet scent. She really didn't want the police, other than Dane, getting involved in this.

He leaned against the counter and sipped his drink. "If there is something bothering you, you can talk to me about it."

"Like what?" she asked cautiously. Did he know? Or suspect there was something going on?

"Oh, I don't know. Anything. No matter how small, or what it is."

"OK, thank you." Amy finished her cocoa. "I might call it a night. It's been a long day." She rinsed her cup and put it in the dishwasher. "Good night, Dane."

"Good night, Amy."

The way he spoke her name was unlike anyone else. She closed the door behind her, trying to stop the shiver running down her spine. Dad had always made her feel special, but this, this was something else altogether.

And she liked it.

It was just a shame it could never be.

She headed up to her room, checking on the girls before shutting the door behind her. She crossed to the window, peeking from behind the closed curtains. There was no one there. She was certain she'd misinterpreted the man from before. Maybe he was merely escorting children trick or treating. Or going to a party. Not spying on her.

Maybe...

12

Monday arrived with no more harassing calls, but then Dane had made a point of answering the phone whenever it rang. Jodie went off to school, with her phone and a grin and a promise not to use it. Amy walked Vicky to school, noticing the child's steps grew slower and slower the closer they got.

They reached the gate, and Vicky stopped. She shook her head, signing frantically and crying.

Amy couldn't keep up, but could guess that it was something about not wanting to go to school. "I know, sweetie, but those girls aren't going to be here this week, remember?"

Pastor Jack and Lara appeared next to them. "Good morning."

Amy looked up. "Morning."

"Problems?" he asked, seeing Vicky's tears.

"She doesn't want to go to school. I can understand it, but she can't stay off."

Lara looked at Vicky, gently touching her arm. "Daddy tolth me they pick on you," she said slowly.

Vicky nodded.

"Me too, becawth I can't talk pwopewy. Maybe we pway with eath othew, and pwotect eath othew fwom the bad giwlth."

Vicky nodded.

Lara held out a hand, smiling as Vicky took it.

Amy looked at Pastor Jack. "Thank you."

"It was Lara's idea. Her speech is a lot better than it was. She still has problems with her R's and a couple of other letters, along with a slight lisp, but since I married Cassie, she's really worked with her and it's improved in leaps and bounds. As soon as I said Vicky was being bullied too, Lara decided they should band together and join forces against the bullies."

Amy smiled. "It's a great idea."

Vicky tugged on Amy's hand and waved.

"Bye, sweetie. See you after school." She watched the girls head in to the playground.

"So how are you?" Pastor Jack asked. "I didn't get a chance to ask you yesterday after the service."

"I'm OK."

"Are you sure?"

She nodded, knowing she wasn't fooling him. "Yeah. I just overreacted on Friday. Thank you again for coming when you did. And for fixing my wrist and the curtain pole."

"You're welcome." He pulled up his collar against the wind. "Jodie rang me. Apparently Dane told her to. We wouldn't have been much longer anyway. Lara had been champing at the bit to come over all day. She'd have been 'round at nine in the morning if we'd let her." His phone rang. "Excuse me."

Amy nodded. She glanced across the road, taking in the cars parked there. No black ones like back in Filely, but that didn't mean he wasn't there watching her. He could have changed his car.

"Can I give you a lift home?"

"Thank you, but no. It's not far and it's a nice day." She began walking, sliding her hands into her pockets, keeping an eye on the traffic. Pastor Jack was very much like Ray. A man full of the spirit of the Lord which bubbled over into everything he said and did. That made her think of Rosalie and the baby. She'd promised she'd be there and she wasn't. She was hundreds of miles away. In fear for her life. And probably going to pull Dane and the girls into the mess she'd made as well.

A black car passed. She increased speed, her heart pounding. Reaching the house, she ran up the path and let herself in, locking the front door before deactivating the burglar alarm. She pulled all the curtains at the front of the house. Was she putting them in danger by being here? Should she leave? What would they do if she did? They needed her.

But more importantly she needed them. And with her feelings for Dane growing, how would she live without them?

❧❦

Dane pulled his swivel chair closer to the desk and put on his thick rimmed reading glasses. Glancing over at Nate, he then brought up the internet window and clicked on the search engine. He flexed his fingers, cracking his knuckles and then began typing.

"What are you doing?" Nate asked.

"Looking something up."

"No, really?"

Dane looked over the top of his glasses at him. "What is it with you today? You have been in a funny mood since you got in."

"Since Friday actually, but you're too stressed to have noticed."

Dane pulled a face at him. He turned back to the computer and peered at it through his glasses. After this he needed to ring the gas board.

"Maybe you should get your eyes tested again."

"Maybe you should do some work," he retorted.

"I'd rather tell you why I'm in a funny mood."

"I'd rather you work and let me get on," Dane said.

Nate rolled his eyes and picked up the file from his desk. "Fine. We got the tox screen results back on the Clarkdale murder. It tested positive for crack..."

Dane tuned him out as he read the screen. Pastor Ray Malone. Several listed but only one in the UK. He clicked on the link. He was pastor of Hillsdale Christian Fellowship, in Filely, North Yorkshire. The church website had a short biography along with a picture of him, his wife and baby. He slowly perused the rest of the site, looking at the photos posted showing some of the congregation.

"'And the cow ran away with the spoon,'" Nate said, more than a hint of exasperation in his tone.

Dane glanced over. "Actually the cow jumped over the moon. It was the dish that eloped with the spoon."

"I didn't think you were listening." Nate scooted his chair across the short space between desks. "What's so interesting?"

"Amy mentioned some friends the other night at dinner. It sounded like they were close, but she hasn't been in touch since she started working here."

"Maybe she has her reasons."

"Maybe. Anyway I thought I'd look them up. See if maybe once I find them, I can convince Amy to contact them. Or ring or email them on her behalf, find out what went wrong between them. Try to help her like she helped us."

Nate glanced at the screen. "I know him. Ray Malone. We met at the London Men's Convention in April. He's a really great bloke. That's a cute baby, too. Love the name Sara."

"Cute babies have a nasty habit of growing into stroppy teenage wannabees."

"Tell me about it. But there's nothing wrong with babies."

Dane leaned back in his chair, giving Nate and his file his full attention. "So...the tox screen tested positive for crack?"

The smile vanished from Nate's eyes and he turned back to the file in his hand, slowly flicking through the pages. "Yes, crack. And not your common or garden variety either. This mix was responsible for a spate of ODs up north about six months ago."

"Whereabouts up north?"

"Would you believe Filely?"

Dane looked at the screen. He hated coincidences. "No, I wouldn't."

"Anyway, the Guv wants us to go up there to check it out."

"Us?" Surely he hadn't heard right.

"Yeah, the two of us. That's you and me. We leave tomorrow, and come back either Thursday night or Friday morning."

"But the girls..."

"The girls will be fine. You have a live-in nanny remember. Besides, it might not take that long. We might be able to wrap it up in a day and leave Wednesday. We'll take a pool car, that way we can both drive and we're not using our cars for work purposes."

"A pool car is fine." He looked at the computer

and shut the window. "The girls won't like me going away. And with stuff escalating at Maranatha Farm…"

"The girls will live. Like I said, you have Amy now. And we won't be gone long. Besides, I really don't want to go away right now either, not with Adeline the way she is, but we don't have a choice. It's our case. Maybe this is why God sent you Amy."

Dane scrawled *ring gas board re reading meter and bill* on a note and looked at him. "Other than to help the girls?"

Nate nodded. "Yeah. Figured if we leave at half six tomorrow morning, we can be there by nine or ten at the latest."

"Sounds good to me." Dane drew in a deep breath. "OK, what's going on? Is Adeline sick?"

"What gives you that idea?"

"Hospital visits. Plus your veiled references to not wanting to leave her alone right now and being in a funny mood for days. And she wasn't in church Sunday morning."

Nate grinned. "Mornings aren't so great right now. But it'll wear off in a few months."

Dane knew the grin on his face mirrored his friend's as the penny dropped. "She isn't?"

"She is. Ten weeks."

Dane pushed his chair back and hugged Nate hard. "Congratulations. Have you told Vianne yet?"

"Not yet. So don't tell the girls, please."

"I won't." Dane grinned. "Good on you."

❦

Jodie looked at him in horror. "You're going away?"

Dane tried to placate her, which wasn't easy at the best of times. When she got in a tizzy, her head very nearly did come off and do a three-hundred-and-sixty-degree turn. "Uncle Nate and I are because of *work*," he emphasized. "My case is connected to one up on the north coast, so Uncle Nate and I have to go up there for a couple of days to compare notes with the officers there."

"You know, Dad, these days you don't need to leave the office at all. You see, there's this really handy invention called the *telephone*. You use it to talk to people. Sometimes even people on the other side of the world. And there's another, even cleverer one called *e-mail*. You can send files thousands of miles with that one."

He shook his head. "Miss Clever Clogs. Sometimes you just have to pound the pavement and do a bit of old-fashioned policing."

Jodie rolled her eyes and put her hands on her hips. "Old-fashioned as in beat a confession out of them, then? A bit of the old 'come with me son, have a cup of tea, kick in the head'…"

Dane scowled. "That's enough. We don't work like that and you know it. You know very well what modern policing entails. You've seen enough on the TV without living with a police officer to know that."

"Yeah, any potential boyfriend runs a mile as soon as he finds out you're a cop, cuz they all think you carry a gun all the time," she said. "And as for pounding the pavements? Shouldn't that be pounding the beaches if you're going to the seaside?"

"Beaches, too, but its November and cold."

"What about the bonfire? You won't be here and Amy doesn't drive," Vicky signed.

"We'll be back before Saturday. Probably be home by Thursday or Friday at the latest. We won't miss the bonfire, I promise."

Jodie folded her arms over her chest and pouted, as only a teenager wannabee could do.

Vicky signed furiously at him.

He grabbed her hands gently. "Honey, I know you don't want me to go, but I'm not leaving you alone. Amy is here. You can text me. I'll call you each night and I *will* be back."

Tears ran down her face, and Dane felt horrible. He wrapped his arms tightly around her. Maybe he was wrong to leave. He looked up at Amy. "I'm trusting you with them."

She nodded. "They'll be fine. We'll all be fine."

"OK."

"Where are you going?"

"Filely."

Her head jerked up to look at him. A haunted expression filled her eyes before she covered it quickly. Her hand rose to fiddle with her necklace.

"Do you know the town?"

"A little," she said.

"Anyway, it's work-related and not a fun excursion."

Jodie scowled. "It's not fair you're going to the beach and we're not. We didn't even have a holiday this year."

"You have to go to school." He paused. "How about we go to Bournemouth in a couple of weeks' time for the day? We could go on a Saturday. You and Vicky can build sandcastles and Amy and I can freeze watching you."

"Cool."

He nodded. "OK. Next weekend, because it's the bonfire this Saturday. And if you're good I'll try to book a weekend away before Christmas. Would you like to go to London or—"

"Bournemouth," Jodie said immediately.

"I was thinking for a weekend we could go to London. See the lights, see the dinosaur museum, go to Hamleys and do some shopping, but if you'd rather go to the beach..."

"London," Jodie said.

Dane grinned as Vicky signed the same thing. "OK then. Beach next weekend and London before Christmas."

"But I'm not sharing a room with you," Jodie said. "Get two rooms then Vicky and I can share with Amy. Cause she can't share your room anyway because you're not married."

He looked at her. "Exactly."

Amy shook her head. "I don't know."

Jodie turned puppy dog eyes on her. "Please, you have to come. I'm too old to share with Dad now. And anyway, he snores."

"I do not," he protested.

"Do too," Jodie argued. "Can Amy come?"

"If she wants to. It's up to her. She might want the weekend off."

She looked from him, back to Amy. "Please come. You have too."

"We'll see."

Dane nodded. "Anyway, it's late and you both have school tomorrow. I'll take you both up. Say 'night to Amy."

"'Night, to Amy," Jodie said, obediently.

Vicky signed it.

"'Night girls."

He came back down half an hour later. Amy was nowhere to be found. He pulled the curtains in the study and paused. There was a man standing opposite the house, dressed in black, just staring at him. He was about to go outside when the bloke got into his car and drove away. Puzzled, he pulled the curtains and turned around jotting down what he could see of the license plate number before heading back into the hall.

Amy descended the stairs, her hair wet. "They go down all right?"

"Yeah. Do me a favor while I'm away."

"Yes, I'll take care of the girls. I'll lock up properly. I've lived on my own for years. I know what to do."

He put a hand on the side of her face, the pad of his thumb rubbing her lips. What was it about her that set his once broken heart aflame? "I didn't mean that. I know you'll take care of the girls."

Her eyes fixed on him, her hand caressed the back of his neck. "Then what did you mean?"

He leaned closer. "Take care of yourself. Because I'm rather fond of you."

"I'm rather fond of you, too."

"Actually," he lowered his voice, the husky tone surprising him. "I'm more than fond of you." He crushed her against him, kissing her.

13

Amy returned from taking Vicky to school, letting herself into the empty house. She wasn't sure if she were relieved or not. It was Thursday. Dane had been gone two days and time just dragged without him around. Not that she saw him during the day, but the evenings were lonely. It wasn't simply his kisses either. His deep voice, the way his presence filled the room, even the way he pushed his hand through his hair as he spoke, made her feel content and safe.

Safe —

Something she wasn't. At least, not any more. She was convinced there was someone watching the house and following her. Or the woman across the road now had a lodger with a dog, because it wasn't her husband hanging around outside every evening. And there seemed to be an awful lot of black cars in Headley Cross all of a sudden.

Or she was simply paranoid.

She deadlocked the front door and decided to distract herself with cleaning. She'd do the entire house, along with changing all the bed sheets and towels.

Dane normally did his own room, but today she'd do it for him, along with his bathroom and the rest of upstairs. After lunch she'd do downstairs. That way if he did come home tomorrow, the house would be spotless.

Amy carried the hoover upstairs and set it down on the landing. She bent to plug it in and then slowly pushed open Dane's bedroom door. She'd never been in there before and for various reasons it felt like violating some inner sanctum.

A noise from the other end of the hall distracted her. Was that coming from her room? She made her way down the hall and pushed open the door. Of course the room was empty. She let out the breath she didn't realize she'd been holding. The book she'd been reading had slid off the bedclothes to the floor. That's what the noise was. She bent to pick it up.

Thudddddd…..

Something hit the window. Amy jumped.

She glanced up. And screamed.

Something red had splattered over the glass. It cast an eerie glow over the entire room. The car accident came to the forefront of her mind.

She wrapped her arms around her middle, her heart pounding. She moved slowly to the window. She would clean it, erase every reminder. Hopefully it would come off easily. She opened the window. Tilt and turn, they either opened on a bottom hinge or like a door so there was a fire exit from each room.

The smell hit her instantly and her stomach turned.

Blood.

A dead bird lay on the ground below the window, a feather stuck to the blood on the window sill.

An innocent "meow" came from the tree and the neighbor's cat peered at her from a branch at the same level as her window. Clamping a hand over her mouth, she dashed for the bathroom.

☙❧

Dane sat on a bench on the promenade, overlooking a very cold beach in Filely, both hands wrapped securely around his coffee, trying to gain every ounce of heat from it he could. And to think the kids had wanted to come with him. He glanced sideways at Nate who looked just as cold as he did. "We should be working."

"We are working. It's called a coffee break while waiting for a contact to show up."

"*If* he shows. And I meant working in a nice warm office. Not wasting time on a freezing cold beach."

Nate's breath hung in the frigid air. "Not putting in for a transfer then?"

"No way. Don't care how much the girls beg." He sipped his coffee.

"Jake Bennett said they'd be here. Just don't forget he's under cover."

"Yeah, well there is cover, deep cover, and being in over your head."

Nate looked at him. "You believe the rumors?"

"No smoke without..." Dane broke off, shrugged, and looked out over the water. Someone was coming. He changed the subject. "There's meant to be a vicious tide here."

A homeless person, bundled in ragged layers pushing a shopping trolley full of bags, stopped next to him. Her face was dirty, her fingernails torn and black and her hair could have been any color originally. She looked at him. "It is. The bodies of those washed away are never found."

"Oh?"

She nodded. She leaned on the handle of the

trolley, her coat rustling against the bags. "Like that young girl several weeks back. She went into the water and got swept away. They said she'd gone swimming. Not the first, won't be the last."

"I see."

"Left all her stuff on the beach."

Nate nodded. "Well if she'd gone swimming, she would have done."

"Mayhap she did, mayhap she didn't. This girl was different, criminal she was. Huge fuss made at the church, even so. Big service for her."

"A funeral," Dane said. "Always happens after a death."

"Not without a body. They never find them." She straightened and pushed the trolley, heading off along the prom.

Dane exchanged a long glance with Nate. "OK, no swimming, then."

Nate sipped his coffee. "No. If I got swept out to sea, Adeline would never speak to me again. Have you heard from Amy?"

"No. Hundreds of texts from the kids though."

Nate shot him a sly glance over the coffee. "Did you kiss her goodbye?"

"That is none of your business."

Nate chuckled. "That's a yes, then."

Dane sipped his coffee. "Company at five o'clock."

Two figures slowly walked across the sand towards them. Both wore leather jackets and jeans, with hiking boots. One had short dark hair, the other a long ponytail. What was it about bad guys and ponytails? Was it listed in the *Bad Guy Handbook*? Always wear leather and have greasy hair in a ponytail?

"Gents," Jake Bennett spoke quietly. "We need to make sure you're not carrying before we go any further."

Dane sighed. "Just the coffee." He set it down and stood. "But I want the same assurance from you two. I have no desire to get shot any time soon."

"We have to make this fast."

Dane nodded. "How do I know you're not wired and the cops aren't listening in?"

"How do I know you're not a cop," the other man replied.

Dane scowled. "I have no time for cops." He spread his arms. "But if you want to check."

He stood still while they patted him down. Then he watched as they did the same checks on Nate.

"OK, we're clean, now it's your turn." He patted down the other two men and then nodded. "Now, can we talk business?"

"How did you hear about me?" The tall man with a ponytail spoke.

"My supplier got nicked. I looked around. Your name came up. Apparently you're one of the best. Your stuff is as good as it comes."

"How much are we talking here?"

"That depends how much and how fast. I have customers waiting and that is bad for business."

"I can let you have two kilos, pure with added kick. It comes in pill form and can be made to your own specifications. Street value, double or treble what you pay me. It can be ready day after tomorrow."

"So what's in it for you?" Dane asked.

"You won't need another supplier. And I establish myself down south. It's a win-win situation."

"I'll need a sample."

The man nodded. "Five hundred. For ten pills."

Dane baulked. "That's too much. Forget it." He turned to Nate. "Let's go."

"Wait." The man stood in front of him. "Four hundred, no less."

Dane handed over the cash and pocketed the plastic bag of pills. "I'll be in touch." He turned his attention back to his coffee, signifying the meeting was over. He raised his cup and sipped slowly, watching the waves pound onto the beach.

The two men left.

Dane didn't say anything until he could no longer see them. "So that's Saunders."

"Well, the brother. Rumor has it, the older one has the entire town in his pocket, along with being the mayor. Cops, judges, the works."

"This isn't Chicago and he's not Al Capone. That just doesn't happen here." Dane finished his coffee and crumpled the cup in his hand.

"Like you said, there's no smoke without fire."

"Yeah, well. Should head back home, get this to the lab." He stood.

"And if it matches?" Nate finished his coffee, putting the cup in the bin.

"Let the others take the glory and celebrate taking one more bad guy off the streets."

Nate nodded his agreement. "I'd drink to that, only the coffee's gone. Do you mind if we call in on the Malone's on the way? I'd like to give Ray my congrats on the baby."

"Sure. I also need to present shop." He began walking to where the car was parked.

"You should have done it yesterday."

"Oh, I got the girls' ones," Dane said. He winked.

"There's one more to get."

Nate laughed. "Come on, we can get it on the way."

❧❦

Amy picked up Vicky from school and then walked to the secondary school to collect Jodie.

Jodie cringed when she saw her. "Oh, please. I walk myself home."

"Not tonight," Amy said firmly.

Jodie shoved her hands into her blazer pockets. "This is so embarrassing. No one else's mother picks them up. I'm in year eight now."

"Yeah, well, I'm not your mother."

"Or their nanny."

Amy refused to give in. "Come on. Sooner you stop arguing, the sooner we're home."

Vicky tugged at her and signed. "Can we go to the park?"

"Not tonight, we're going straight home."

She signed again.

Amy shook her head. "I didn't catch any of that."

"Is Daddy coming home tonight?" Jodie translated.

"I don't think so. It's more likely to be tomorrow rather than tonight now. Or if it is tonight it'll be long after you're in bed and asleep."

Jodie groaned. She pulled out her phone and dialed. "Dad? Yeah, Amy's being mean. She's picking me up from school like a baby, and she won't take us to the park tonight."

Amy raised an eyebrow and shook her head as she walked.

Jodie's tone became indignant. "No, I'm not acting like a baby. When are you coming home?" She paused. "Oh." She thrust the phone at Amy. "He wants to talk to you."

Amy took a deep breath. "Hello."

"Hey Amy." Dane's voice thrilled her, making her hair stand on end. Almost as if he were caressing her. "How are you?"

"I'm fine. Aside from being an ogre tonight, apparently. I might have to change my name to the green cross woman."

"So I gather. And the name change sounds good. She'll live."

"I hope so. They miss you."

"I miss them. Should be back tomorrow, just got a couple more things to do up here. Might even drive back tonight, we'll have to see how it goes. I got to go. Give Vicky my love—" There was a squeal of brakes and the line went dead.

Vicky held out her hand, her face falling as Amy gave the phone back to Jodie.

"He got cut off. He did send his love though. Said he'll be back either late tonight or tomorrow during the day. We should go home, it's getting dark."

"Not for an hour yet." Jodie pouted.

Amy dropped it and changed the subject. This was by far the best way to deal with Jodie at times. What she'd do when Jodie figured that one out, she wasn't sure. But for now the plan worked every time. "What do you want for dinner?"

"Pizza."

"Want to help make it?"

Both girls nodded.

"OK. Come on then."

❧❧

Dane slowly pushed himself up from the dash. His chest hurt where he'd been thrown into the seatbelt as Nate had performed an emergency stop to avoid hitting the car that suddenly stopped in front of them.

"Are you OK?" Nate asked.

Dane nodded, mentally doing a once over. "I'm fine. What about you?"

"Fine."

"Uh oh, trouble." Dane nodded as a man leapt from the car and rushed towards a woman pushing a pram.

The man pulled a gun from his jacket and pointed at the woman, yelling at her to move away from the pram. The woman shook her head, holding the pram tightly.

The man grabbed her arm, pulling at her.

Nate looked out of the window. "So, do we dial 9-9-9 and call it in or go be heroes? Bear in mind he's armed and we're not."

"We go be heroes, of course. Silly question." Dane grinned. "Call it in after."

He opened the car door and stepped out. "Everything all right?" he asked, walking carefully over to the gunman.

"Don't move." The gunman pointed the gun at him. "Just leave. This doesn't concern you."

Dane nodded to the woman. She looked familiar, but he couldn't place where he'd seen her before. "And it does her? Just let her go."

The gunman pointed the gun at the woman's head. "I said leave. She and I have unfinished business." He broke the woman's hold on the pram and dragged her with him towards the car.

The woman screamed, reaching for the pram, heedless for her own safety. "Not my baby! Sara!"

Dane didn't back down, aware of Nate circling around behind the gunman. He grabbed the pram, pulling it safely behind him. "Then why don't you just sit down and talk about it. Hurting her isn't going to accomplish anything other than you getting into trouble. You let the baby go, now let her go and we can sort this out."

The man pushed the woman into the car. "I said back off. It's none of your business."

Nate moved in fast to disarm him, but the man fired first.

Pain shot through Dane's shoulder, and he fell against the car, clutching it. Stars danced before his eyes, and he glanced down. Blood seeped through his fingers.

Salt stung his eyes.

His knees buckled.

A car drove away at full speed.

A voice echoed his name. "Dane... Dane...You stay with me, mate...Help's on the way, just stay with me..."

Faces swam in front of him, slowly at first, then faster, almost on a carousel.

Jas...Jodie...Vicky...Nate...Amy...

Everything went black.

14

Dane sat on the bed in the ED and looked at Nate. "How much longer do we have to sit here?"

"I have no idea. Until the doc says you're good to go, we have to stay put. I really am sorry."

"Stop apologizing. If I got a quid for every time you've done that in the last hour or so, I'd be able to retire."

"Sorry."

"Stop it. You did what you had to do."

"And got you shot." Nate looked down at his hands. "He got away and took the woman with him. At least the baby's safe. Baby's fine, by the way. She's up on the children's ward until the local boys trace her father."

"And you saw the number of the car and descriptions of all of them. He won't get far. And being hurt in the line of duty happens."

"I got you shot. I'm sorry, I feel horrible."

"You feel horrible?" Dane rolled his eyes. "You'll feel even worse when I start charging you for apologizing. Did you pull the trigger? No. Therefore it's not your fault."

"But—"

"Nate," he said, totally exasperated now. "Enough. No buts. I'm going to be fine. 'Sides, you owed me."

"Huh?"

"I punched you the other week and laid you out in the car park. Remember, you told me to count my blessings, so I said one and decked you. Then you made that stupid comment about at least I didn't do it in front of the Guv."

"Oh, that."

"Yeah, that. So call it quits and forget about it. I'm sorry we didn't get to see your friend."

"I'll ring him later."

The curtain opened. "Can't you two stay out of trouble for five minutes?"

Dane looked up. That wasn't who he was expecting to see. "Guv?"

DI Welsh smiled slightly. "In the flesh. How are you doing?"

"Sore, but I'll live. It missed anything vital and went straight through. How did you find out?"

"Nate rang, a few minutes before the local boys did."

"This isn't Nate's fault, no matter what he thinks."

"I know. Do you still have the..." Welsh gestured.

Dane nodded. "Yes."

"Good. I'm taking you both back to Headley Cross now. My car is outside."

Nate looked at her. "What about the pool car?"

"The AA will tow it back. It won't work without the spark plugs." She patted her pocket. "You'll come back to the station, and I'll debrief you on this trip and this morning's incident. I don't want you talking to the local boys."

"Guv?" Dane exchanged a puzzled look with Nate.

"I'm pulling strings. You two report to me and no one else."

"With all due respect," Nate began. "Dane's been shot. He needs rest…"

"And he'll get it. But not here and not before I've spoken to you both and got it on the record."

"What about our things?"

"The guest house you were staying in caught fire a couple of hours ago. It looks as if the fire started in your room. Of course, you were both here or on the way here at the time. But I don't like it. I want you out of here ASAP."

"But the doc…" Dane began.

"That's an order, Sergeant. Janice will be waiting at the station to check you over and do anything that needs doing."

Nate shook his head. "And the woman? Do they know who she is yet?"

"They're looking for her. And no, not yet."

An orderly came in with a wheelchair.

"I can walk," Dane protested.

He broke off at the black look that crossed his commanding officer's face. He sat in the chair. What was going on? What had they innocently walked in to?

❧

Morning came all too soon. Amy pulled the lounge curtains and jumped as next door's cat peered in at her. She shook her head as the feline hopped down and walked away, its tail high in the air. A dead mouse lay on the window sill. Amy let out a deep breath. What was wrong with her? She wasn't normally this nervy. Maybe things were just getting too much.

A scream came from the kitchen, and she ran

through the hallway. "What's wrong?"

Jodie pointed, still screaming. A dead bird lay on the windowsill.

"Calm down. It's probably just that menace of a cat."

"Don't have a cat."

"Next door do. It was on the lounge windowsill just now and left a mouse there as well. I'll get rid of the bird and the mouse, just give me a minute."

"Don't touch it."

"I'm not going to." Amy pulled a plastic carrier bag from the drawer and went outside. She carefully slid her hand into the wrong side of the bag and picked up the bird without touching it. "See, not a problem." She moved across the garden and picked up the mouse as well.

Jodie screamed again making Amy jump.

"Now what?"

Jodie pointed to a dead squirrel.

Amy sighed. "Just let me get rid." She scooped it up in the same bag and then sealed it. She put it into the dustbin and went inside to wash her hands thoroughly. She looked out over the back garden as she did. Gold, red and yellow leaves lay scattered across the otherwise empty lawn. This time of year was so pretty, but so untidy.

The doorbell rang. Jodie looked over. "I'll get it."

"Thank you." Amy finished washing her hands and then reached for the towel.

Jodie came back in with a huge bunch of flowers. "They're for you."

She took them. "I wonder who sent them."

"Probably Dad."

"Why would your father be sending me flowers?"

She flicked Jodie's nose. "Have you got everything?"

"Yes I have. And my food tech stuff. We're making bread this afternoon. There's a card. Can I read it?"

"I'll read it when I get back. We should go or we're going to be late." She put the flowers on the counter and headed out to get the coats. "Come on, Vicky," she yelled up the stairs.

Jodie followed her. "Who's Kevin?" she asked holding out the card.

"I don't know a Kevin," Amy said. "And you shouldn't open other people's mail."

"I just thought they might be from Dad. What does 'condolences' mean?"

"It means being sorry for something."

"OK, so what did Kevin do wrong that he had to buy you flowers to say sorry for."

Amy sighed. "I told you, I don't know a Kevin. Let's go."

She took the card from Jodie and shoved it by the telephone.

She walked the girls to school, and waited until Vicky had gone in, before letting her mind run over the flowers. She only knew of one Kevin, and he wanted her dead. But why would he be sending her flowers and how did he know where she was? Was everything else that was happening connected? Was he trying to intimidate her? Or scare her? Because if that was his intention, then he'd succeeded.

The bad feeling in her gut grew as she got closer to the house. Her heart sank as she saw more blood coating the door. This time spelling her name. That definitely was not the work of the cat. And a little sick for a mere schoolboy crush.

She quickly cleaned it off and then deadlocked the

front door. She picked up the card and read it, the hair standing on the back of her neck. She shivered and set the burglar alarm before she headed into the lounge.

Booting up the laptop, she carried it into the kitchen and set it on the counter. She poured a cup of coffee, sat on the stool, and settled down to watch a cooking show she'd missed the previous evening. The main news page caught her eye and she clicked on the link. Rosalie's picture filled the screen. *Pastor's wife falls from cliff.*

Tears filled her eyes, as her hand rose to her mouth. *Nooooo....*

❧❦

Dane sat quietly as Nate drove him home. It had been a long twenty-four hours. The guv had been relentless with her interviewing, not leaving anything to chance—taking the rest of the night the drive home hadn't. He rubbed his shoulder, the sling restricting all movement in his left arm.

Nate glanced at him. "I wish you'd agreed to time off."

Dane pulled a face. "It's Friday. We're off until Monday anyway. I was wondering if you'd take the girls to the church bonfire tomorrow night."

"What about you and Amy?"

"I can't drive, neither does she. You can't fit all of us in your car. Just take the girls. I can always burn the rubbish in the incinerator if Amy wants a fire."

"Maybe we do that anyway. Or build a bonfire. I can bring fireworks."

"I promised the girls they could go to the church one."

Nate parked outside the house and held his hands up in an expression of defeat. "In that case I'll take them. I'll pick them up at five."

"Thank you." He opened the door. "I'll see you then." He watched Nate drive off, and then headed up the path. He unlocked the door and stepped over the lintel.

The alarm started beeping. "What the..." Maybe Amy was out. He deactivated it and hung his coat on the rack. Something fell in the kitchen.

"Amy?"

No answer.

"Amy, is that you?"

He headed to the kitchen and pushed open the door. Amy sat on the stool, tears streaking her face, totally distraught. Running across the room, he pushed the laptop to one side, before sitting beside her and wrapping his good arm around her. What could have happened this time? He held her tightly as she sobbed. "Lord, I don't know what's upsetting Amy right now, but You do. Be close to her, comfort her."

He glanced at the laptop, and his heart skipped a beat. Shock flooded him, twisting his stomach into a hard knot. "Noooo—"

He pulled his phone from his pocket, stifling the gasp of pain. He speed-dialed Nate.

The phone rang five times before Nate answered. He could hear the indicator ticking and the car engine in the background. "Holmes."

"Nate, it's me." Dane took a deep breath. "Sorry to make you pull over."

"Are you missing me already?" Amusement filled Nate's voice.

"Something's happened." He let his tone convey

urgency, knowing his partner would pick up on it.

"You need me to come back?"

"Ye…" His voice cracked. "Yes."

"What's up?" Nate's tone turned concerned yet professional.

"Ray Malone's wife was killed yesterday. Fell off the cliff according to the news."

"Hang on. You're saying she committed suicide?"

"It doesn't say, just that she went over the cliff. But there are references to postnatal depression." He drew in a deep calming breath. "Nate…"

"What?"

"Just get back here, pronto."

"On my way."

Ten minutes later, Nate's car pulled up on the drive. Dane left Amy long enough to let him in. She'd stopped crying, just sat leaning against him, pale and drawn, staring at a bunch of flowers next to the laptop.

Dane took Nate's coat, kicking the door shut with his foot.

Nate didn't bother with the niceties of hello. "Ray's wife? Are you sure?"

"It's on the news. Amy was upset when I got home. The article still up."

Nate followed Dane into the kitchen. "Amy…"

"Hi, Nate." She looked up from ripping a tissue to shreds.

Dane sat and wrapped his arm around her again.

Nate stopped at the breakfast bar and pulled the laptop across. It didn't take his partner long to make the connection that he had. "That's her. I don't believe this. We were there. We should have stopped this from happening. You reckon they killed her?"

"That's what I'm thinking."

"Maybe if we'd gone to see Ray sooner, we could have stopped her from leaving."

"We were on the way there," Dane reminded him. "But like you said in the hospital, at least we saved the baby." But even that felt a hollow victory now.

"I just don't believe what I'm seeing." Nate looked back at the screen. "Postnatal depression...but even so..."

"You know Ray?" Amy asked quietly.

Nate nodded. "Yes, I do. I met him in London back in April. We've kept in touch on and off ever since."

"I went to university with Rosalie. She was all I had and now, now I don't have anyone." She dissolved into sobs again.

Dane closed his eyes, his face creasing with pain as Amy moved against his chest.

"You need more pain meds?" Nate asked.

"It might be an idea."

"Where are they?"

"Still in my coat pocket, which is hanging in the hall." Dane nodded to the door.

Nate stood. "I'll get them."

Amy looked up. "Pain meds?" Her eyes widened as she took in the sling for the first time. "You're hurt? Why didn't you say anything?"

"You were upset. I didn't want to worry you further."

"What happened?"

"I got shot. It's a very long, boring story, not worth repeating."

The color drained from her face. "Dane..."

"It's fine. Few weeks and I'll be fighting fit and back to scaling fences again." He kissed her cheek softly. "I promise, I'm OK." Her fingers gently traced his collar bone, making him wince. Then hiss.

"Sorry." She moved her hand.

"It's fine. It's a clean wound, just a little uncomfortable."

Nate appeared beside him, holding out a glass of water and the pills. "Here."

He took them. "Thank you." He looked at Amy. "So, short story is I'll live. Who are the flowers from?"

She shrugged. "They came before I left to take the kids to school."

Nate picked up the card. "'Dearest Amy. With sincere condolences. Kevin.' Kevin who?"

"I don't know." Amy shivered. "No one knows I live here."

"But you knew Rosalie."

"Yes. But no one knows I live *here*," she repeated. "I haven't spoken to Ray or Rosalie in weeks."

Dane looked at her, trying to work this out in his mind. "You didn't give them this address?"

Her voice rose. "I told you. No one has it. No one knows I'm here."

"Well, someone obviously does."

"I haven't told anyone, why would I? And you can't go telling Ray where I am either."

"Why ever not? If you were as close as you say you were, you should ring him. He's going to need every friend he can get right now."

She pushed up. "I have my reasons. You can't tell him, please."

Surprise filled him. "It's OK."

"Not OK. Never OK." Her voice rose, her agitation tangible. "Please, promise me you won't tell him I'm here. You can't."

"All right, we won't say anything." Dane reached

for her, but she pulled away and ran from the room. He sat there stunned.

"Well, that was weird," Nate said quietly.

"Yeah, right."

"Did you ever do a background check on her?"

"I didn't think I needed to."

"Maybe you should."

Dane drew in a deep breath, trying to ignore the growing nausea. "Why? Because I'm falling for her? Because she's my daughters' nanny?"

Nate shook his head. "No. Because she knew Rosalie. Someone sent her flowers the day after we saw Rosalie Malone kidnapped and she winds up dead. She jumped off a cliff because of screwed-up hormones? I doubt that very much—not the way she reacted when that guy grabbed her. Then there are the phone calls Amy got."

"Not since the number was changed."

The phone rang three times and stopped as Dane picked it up. "Amy must have gotten it." He put the phone down again.

It rang again, and then stopped.

Nate raised an eyebrow. "You were saying?"

It rang a third time. Then stopped. Dane stood. "OK, this is beyond a joke now." He moved to the door. "Amy? Who was on the phone?"

"It was a wrong number. I'm going for a shower."

"OK, but let me get it next time." He went back into the kitchen.

Nate stood by the kitchen window and glanced over his shoulder at him. "I didn't think you were doing a bonfire this year."

Dane shook his head, rubbing his arm. It really hurt now, not that he was going to admit it to anyone.

"I'm not. We already discussed this. You're taking the girls to the church one. Amy and I are staying here."

Nate nodded to the garden. "Then what's that?"

"I don't know. You tell me." Dane turned to the window. "What the…"

A huge bonfire made of twigs, leaves and branches sat in the middle of the lawn. A scary looking guy made of black cloth with a red wig, and dark red cricket balls for eyes rested on the top.

He swallowed. "I don't remember it being there."

"Maybe the kids built it while we were up north."

"No, I mean that wasn't there when I got home. I'm sure it wasn't. And no one's been outside. The kids are at school, and I've been in here with Amy. I would have noticed a bonfire and a guy that scary." He pulled his mobile from his pocket and, pulling up the camera app, snapped several photos.

The landline phone rang again. Dane answered it. If this was another prank call, he was getting the line traced, no matter what Amy wanted. He didn't say anything, not wanting to tip the caller off that it wasn't Amy answering the phone.

Heavy breathing hissed in his ear, followed by a husky voice. "Burn in hell, Amy."

The bonfire in the garden exploded.

15

Amy watched from the kitchen window as Dane put the fire out with the hose one handed. She'd heard the shouts from upstairs and gotten to the landing window in time to see them both bolt outside. Nate raked over the embers to ensure the flames were completely out and no sparks were left to reignite later on.

She couldn't stay here. She was putting everyone in danger. He'd probably gotten shot because of her. There were too many coincidences, and she didn't believe in them on a good day: And this was definitely *not* a good day.

There was the blood, dead critters, phone calls, the man outside the house. And now this. She hadn't built the bonfire. The girls hadn't. And it hadn't been there when she left the house that morning. She knew that because she'd been in the garden clearing up the dead animals.

Why are You letting this happen? Haven't I paid enough without Dane, the girls and now Ray paying for my mistake? I heard what they said about the woman being kidnapped and they thought it was Rosalie. It's my fault. All of it.

The men came in, wiping their feet on the mat. Dane looked right through her as he shut the door. "Well?" he demanded.

Nate leaned against the back door, arms folded

tightly across his chest.

She held Dane's gaze. "Well, what?"

"What are you hiding?"

Amy swallowed nervously, her tongue darting out to lick her lips. "Nothing."

Dane moved over to her, blocking her exit. "Don't give me that. Did you build that bonfire and guy?"

"No."

"Did the girls?"

"No. They wanted to build one, but I said they had to wait until you got home. But as they were going to the church one, there probably wasn't any need to. And besides, I wasn't going to go through your clothes and give them some. That's up to you."

"So you didn't build the one outside?"

"No, for the third time." She screwed her face up in confusion. "There wasn't one there earlier on."

"Then who did build it?"

"I don't know. I just said there wasn't one before I left to take the girls to school this morning. Next door's cat left a dead bird in the garden. I went out there to remove it. I think I'd have noticed a bonfire."

"Was it there when you got back?"

"I don't know."

"Amy!" Exasperation flooded his voice.

"I don't know. I don't routinely look out the windows to check stuff like that."

"That last call mentioned you by name Then the fire went up outside. That is one awfully big coincidence. Never mind the fact the guy was wearing a long red wig."

Amy turned around, afraid she was going to throw up then and there. She shook hard, wrapping her arms around her middle. "I should just resign and go away before anyone gets hurt."

Dane's right hand gripped her tightly, spinning her around. "That won't help. If you're involved in something, or if there is someone after you for whatever reason, then I need to know. I can stop him."

"I'm not," she whispered. "I told you, I don't know who *he* is."

"What about those previous calls today? Did he say your name?"

"No. Whoever it was didn't say anything. There was no one there."

"You said it was a wrong number."

Nate moved over and put a hand on Dane's arm. "Calm down, Dane. Getting in her face isn't going to help."

Dane stepped back, cradling his arm.

Nate nodded, and then looked at Amy. "Amy, think for a moment. When did the phone calls start again?"

"Today," she whispered. "Just before the fire started."

"Those three calls earlier?" Dane asked.

Nate silenced him with a look. "Is anything else happening?"

She hesitated. "No."

Nate narrowed his eyes. "Because we can't stop it if you don't tell us."

"There isn't," she whispered, looking down. Something prompted her to be honest, but she couldn't. They were cops. Who would they believe? Her or her criminal record? She was a convicted criminal—she wasn't allowed to work with kids. Dane would want her out of his house, away from his kids, away from him. She'd lose everything. Again.

The phone rang, and she jumped, her breath catching in her throat.

Dane snatched it up. "Hello." He listened for a moment. "I'll be there." He hung up. "Vicky fell in PE. They need her to be picked up and checked over at the hospital."

"I'll go and get her," Amy said. She grabbed her bag from the side and left before either of the men could stop her.

❧

Dane growled as Amy shut the door. "I was going with."

"So go with," Nate said. "Just calm down a bit first."

"Don't you tell me to calm down," he snapped. "I'm not going to lose anyone else I love to some maniac with a grudge."

"Then let me call the guv. Get the arson boys over here to check it out."

"Arson?" He opened the door. "Amy, wait up."

Nate lowered his voice. "You said yourself it's not a coincidence, and I don't believe in spontaneous combustion any more than you do. Someone built that fire and the guy. If it wasn't Amy or the girls, then it's someone trying to tell you something. And I'll put a trace on the line."

"Just unplug it."

"And that will do what? Just go with Amy and pick up Vicky. I'll stay here." Nate pulled out his phone. "It's probably best you're not here for this."

Dane headed after Amy. "Amy, I said wait."

"I am waiting." She stood on the path.

He struggled into his coat. "We should take the car in case she needs to get her arm x-rayed. It's a long walk to the hospital."

"You can't drive. Nor can I."

"Do you know how to? Can you drive? Have you passed your test?"

"Yes, but…"

"Then you drive."

"But, Dane…"

What was it with her and answering him back or not answering him at all today? She'd picked the wrong day to wind him up, that's for sure.

He snapped. His home had been hit by an arsonist, he'd been shot, and now his daughter was injured. "It's not up for debate. You drive my car with my permission. Now get in."

Amy reluctantly got in the driver's side and sat still while Dane quickly ran through where everything was. She started the car. "It's been a while."

"You'll be fine. It's like riding a bike. You never really forget. You can park just down from the gates of the school." He leaned back in the seat, cradling his arm.

"Did you mean what you said just now? About not wanting to lose someone you love?"

"You heard that?"

"Yeah, sorry. I didn't mean to overhear, but your voice carried."

"Yes, I meant it. After Jas died, I didn't think I'd ever live or love again. You've shown me otherwise. I love you. I don't want anything happening to you. Which is why *if* you know *anything*, you have to tell me."

"I don't."

"OK."

"What did the school say about Vicky?"

Dane noted the change of subject, but went with it. For now. "She fell off the beam and landed on her arm. One of the kids said they heard a crack. It's swollen, she won't use it, and she screams if someone touches it."

"Screams?" Amy took her eyes off the road long enough to look at him.

"Yeah. This is another reason to worry." He took a deep breath. "Pull in just along here somewhere."

Amy parked and turned off the engine.

Dane leapt out of the car as soon as it stopped moving. He waited for her to catch up with him. The door opened before he could ring the bell, he assumed because they'd seen him coming.

Vicky waited in reception holding her arm and crying. Her teacher sat with her.

Dane knelt beside her, wrapping his good arm around his daughter. "It's OK, honey. Daddy's here now."

Vicky clung to him, sobbing hard.

Miss Macnin looked at him. "I don't think it's broken, but you should go and get it X-rayed just to be on the safe side. It's not like her to make such a fuss." She looked at Vicky and smiled. "Hope you feel better soon."

He nodded. "OK, thank you. Come on, honey. Amy's going to drive us to the hospital, so they can take pictures of your arm, too."

Vicky looked at him, tears running down her red and blotchy face.

Dane pointed to his shoulder. "Uncle Nate took me to the hospital when I hurt my arm and the doctor took lots of pictures with a special camera that can see what your bones look like. Maybe we both get a sling."

❧

Four hours later, they got back to the house. Vicky's arm wasn't broken, just sprained. They'd wrapped it in tubigrip and put her arm in a sling. It meant she'd be back to nodding or shaking her head for a day or two, but Dane could live with that.

Amy parked in the garage, while he took Vicky inside. He hung up her coat and then slid out of his.

Vicky clung to his hand tightly.

Nate sat in the kitchen with Jodie and Vianne. He glanced up as they came in. "Hey, matching slings. Neat."

He tilted his head slightly. "Yeah. It's just a sprain."

Jodie hugged him. "Vicky or you, Dad?"

He hugged her back. "Vicky. Mine's a little more serious than that, but I'll live."

Nate winked at her. "One fence too many in his case. He's not as young as he likes to think he is."

Dane rolled his eyes.

"As long as you're all right, Dad, that's what matters." Then with typical teenage aplomb, Jodie changed the subject. "Can I sleep 'round Vianne's tonight? It's OK with Uncle Nate."

"Sure." That would be one less child for him to worry about right now.

Nate looked at Vicky. "Did you want to come too?"

She shook her head, not letting go of Dane's hand.

"OK. Jodie, go and get your stuff."

Amy came in and put her bag on the counter.

Dane glanced at the window then back at Nate. "Study for a few?"

Nate nodded.

Dane looked at Vicky. "Honey, can you help Amy make Daddy something to drink?"

She nodded slowly.

Dane kissed her forehead and followed Nate from the kitchen. He shut the study door behind them. "Well?"

"It was arson." Nate said without preamble. "But we knew that. They found the remnants of a radio device in the ash."

"How did they get in?"

"The lock on the back gate is broken. It's been fixed now and the bolt moved further down. The girls still can't reach it, but no one can just reach over the fence and open it anymore. You didn't notice anything at all when you got home?"

"No. I was busy with Amy." He paused. "Nothing like that. Stop raising your eyebrows at me. She was really upset, and I rang you within a couple of minutes of getting in."

"OK. We need to speak to her again, then. If it wasn't there before she left for school, it was either done while she was out, or while the three of us were talking."

Dane shuddered at the thought. "The school run takes about twenty minutes. Maybe fifteen minutes longer if she was taking Jodie and Vianne as well. Is that long enough?"

"Maybe, I don't know. Talk to her later on tonight. Then ring me and let me know if she remembers anything."

"Will do."

"Then there are the flowers. I've given the card to Pete to try to trace. Jodie said the flowers arrived before they left for school. Which was *before* Amy found out about Rosalie Malone."

Dane's stomach turned. "It sounds like she's being targeted."

"Or you are. Maybe you should take her away this weekend."

"And go where?" He sighed. "I can't drive. She can, but won't for whatever reason. I practically had to force her to drive to the hospital and back. No, I'll unplug the phone, put the security lights on and get a patrol to drive past a few times."

"Already done. Oh, and the guv said no unplugging the phone. She's put a trace on the line. Right, it sounds as if the girls are ready. Ring if you need anything. Otherwise I will see you tomorrow."

Dane saw him out and went back into the kitchen. Amy leant against the counter, sipping a mug of tea. He stood next to her. "Where's Vicky?"

"She's watching TV in the lounge."

"I need to talk to you about this morning."

"I already told you. The bonfire wasn't there when I left, and I didn't notice it when I got back. I was gone about forty minutes or so."

"Did you lock up the house?"

"Of course, and I set the alarm, just like I always do."

"OK. Nate said the back gate was broken, so that's probably how they got in."

"I'm sorry."

"It's not your fault. Even if this person is after you, it's not your fault. We'll get him." He wrapped his arm around her and gently kissed her cheek.

Amy turned into him at the same moment, grazing his lips.

He needed no more encouragement and kissed her deeply, only breaking off when he felt a tug on his sleeve. He glanced down and smiled. "Hey, Vicks. Are you all right?"

She signed awkwardly.

He nodded. "Yes, I do love her. Is that OK?"

She shot him a thumbs-up and mimed a drink.

Amy nodded. "Sure. Milk?"

Vicky shook her head.

"Juice, then?"

She shook her head.

"Then, what about lemonade? I can do magic lemonade if you like."

Vicky looked confused, but then nodded.

Dane frowned. "*Magic* lemonade? What are you teaching her?"

Amy looked at him and then down. "OK, just plain lemonade, then."

He reached for her, but she sidestepped him. "Amy, I didn't mean to upset you."

"You didn't. It's fine." She poured Vicky a glass. "Here you go." She pulled open the freezer.

"Are you mad at me?" he asked, watching her.

"No." Her tone was as stiff as her stance.

He frowned. Her body language indicated otherwise as she rattled around boxes and oven trays. "Amy?" he tried again. "Talk to me."

She shoved two trays into the oven. "There, shepherd's pie for you and fish fingers and chips for Vicky. And baked beans for the both of you."

"What about you?"

"Not hungry."

"You haven't eaten all day."

She shoved her hands into her pockets, leaning against the counter. "I'm not hungry." Tears slid down her face, before she turned away.

Dane stood behind her, sliding his good arm around her waist. She leaned against him, crying hard. "You have to eat," he whispered.

"No point..."

"There's every point, Amy." He kissed her neck. "I know you're sad and scared, right now. It's been a horrible day."

She nodded.

"I don't want you getting sick from not eating. We need you." He lowered his voice, pulling her closer against him. "I need you."

"You don't know me," she whispered.

"I know I love you."

"Love you, too."

He kissed her gently, feeling her shiver. "Please eat something. Even if it's just soup or toast or that incredibly sugary cereal you insisted on buying." When she glanced at him, he tipped up her chin. "So explain this magic lemonade."

"You put a drop of food coloring into a plastic cup or mug without the child seeing it. Then you show them the bottle of clear lemonade. Pour it into the cup and give it to them. Only of course it's red or blue or green and they sit there wondering how you did it."

"That's neat. We'll have to do it Sunday lunch for the girls. Just need to rename it."

"To what?"

"Something other than magic," he said lightly. "How about enchanted..."

"Or fairy," she said.

"Fairy lemonade," Dane said, kissing her again. "I like the sound of that." He hugged her. "We'll be OK, I promise."

She looked at him. "But everything is so messed up and I can't see how to put any of this right."

"It looks messed up, yes, but it isn't. God is in control. We just need to remember that. And tomorrow, both girls are out at the church bonfire with Nate and Adeline. So, how about you and I take a long walk somewhere. Just the two of us?"

"I'd like that."

16

Dane shut the front door as Adeline picked up Vicky and Jodie to take them to the bonfire. He and Nate had spent most of the day at Maranatha farm as the cult case they were working on escalated and took an unexpected and somewhat nasty turn. Nate was still there and would most likely end up working, rather than watching the fireworks.

Dane had come back home, because Nate insisted. Things at home seemed to be mirroring events on the farm just a little too much for either of them to be comfortable leaving Amy alone.

He looked at Amy. "Alone at last," he grinned.

She shook her head. "Am I safe with you?" she asked. "I mean you climb fences and put handcuffs on people all day long."

He laughed. "That sounds terrible. Put your coat on and we'll get out of here. I thought we could walk to the park, go around the lake and maybe watch the fireworks from there."

"There'll be some here?"

He nodded. "Yes, although we've never been to that display. We always go to the church one."

"You could have gone with them."

"They didn't have room in the car. Besides, it was planned this way because I want to be with you. Without the girls around for once." He kissed her cheek. "So, shall we?"

She nodded. "Sure."

He took her hand and led her from the house, along the dark streets towards the park. At that moment, he knew he had fallen for her, without ever hope of recovering.

He'd seen enough criminals in his long career to know that Amy wasn't one. Her love for God radiated from her, even when she was at her most vulnerable and downcast. And she loved his kids. That was evident from the way she cared for them and had gone the extra mile to help both Vicky and Jodie when they needed it. She wasn't an evil person; she was wonderful and sweet and he couldn't believe God had brought her into his life the way He had.

Whoever it was targeting them had better watch out. Because Amy now rated right alongside his girls in the keep-your-hands-off-them-or-else stakes.

"What are you thinking?" Amy's voice broke into his thoughts.

But there was no way he could tell her his true thoughts. Not yet. Not until all this was sorted out. Instead, he went for the other thing on his mind. "Thinking how nice this is," he said. "Just you and me."

She nodded. "It is. Not that I mind the girls being around. It's just nice that, oh, how do I put this without it sounding bad?"

"Without having to worry about them being safe?"

She smiled. "That's it exactly. Especially with all this stuff going on." Then he felt her stiffen.

"Amy, if you know something, you would tell me, right? Doesn't matter what it is, or how small it may be."

She nodded. "Yeah."

He looked at her, unconvinced, but not going to push it, no matter what his instincts told him. "OK." He ran his gloved fingers over hers, wishing the gloves weren't in the way, but with the temperature actually below freezing, he wasn't going to risk taking them off. His breath froze in front of him, and he tugged his hat down further over his ears.

Amy did the same, pulling her matching red scarf close around her face. "Bet it looks pretty around here when it snows."

"It does. The council isn't very prompt with the gritting lorries though, so driving is a pain for a day or two. But the girls love it, especially when they get a snow day."

"That must be fun. I haven't seen snow since university."

"Didn't you get any in Filely?"

She looked sharply at him. Did he imagine the gasp? "Where?"

"That's where Ray Malone is pastor, right? You said you moved to the same town as him and his wife."

"Oh, yeah, right. We got some, but it never lasted long. Not the way it does in other parts of the country."

He walked with her, their footsteps crunching on the gravel as they entered the park. The moon shone high above them and excited children ran to and fro across the car park, calling to each other. "Did you have bonfires as a child?"

"Yeah. Dad would build one in the garden. We'd never have fireworks, but we had sparklers. And afterwards we'd have fish and chips from the chip shop. What about you?"

"We'd go to the local display. They'd do soup, hotdogs, and jacket potatoes."

"I love those. Jacket potatoes that is." Her eyes lit up. "I haven't had a proper one in years. Ones covered in butter and grated cheese, cooked for a good two hours in the oven. With the skin all crispy and the inside so hot it burns your mouth and lips."

Dane grinned. "A woman after my own heart. Only I want a jacket potato now."

"When we get home."

"But I don't want to wait two hours."

Amy laughed. "You sound like Jodie. That must be where she gets it from."

He pouted. "I do not sulk either."

"Do too."

"Do not."

She elbowed him. "Do too and are now." She grinned. "But you look so cute when you do."

Dane turned to face her. "Cute?"

Amy tugged his hat right down over his face. "Even cuter now."

He pulled the hat back and looked indignantly at her. It didn't have the desired effect as she just dissolved into giggles. "Oh, really?"

"Yes, really," she managed.

He tugged her hat down over her face. "Big improvement."

"Oy."

"Something wrong?" He grinned as she pushed her hat back.

"Yes. You."

"Me?" He wrapped his arm around her and pulled her close. "How about now?"

Amy leaned against him. "Much better."

He kissed her forehead, mindful of the fact that they were in public. He didn't want word getting back to the girls. Yes, they knew, or at least Vicky did, but he didn't want to give anyone else the wrong idea. Not yet anyway.

As they stood by the lake, fireworks exploded over their heads, the colors reflecting in the still water. Amy looked up. "Wow. So pretty."

"Like you," Dane whispered, pulling her close. She made his life complete, something he never thought it would be again.

ॐৡ

Monday came with no more incidents, but Amy put that down to the fact Dane had once more made his presence felt all over the weekend, both inside and outside the house. Once he'd gotten back from work on Saturday afternoon, that is. He'd mowed the lawn one handed both front and back, before helping the girls build a scarecrow after lunch on Sunday. Albeit under duress, but despite his constant complaining to wind up the girls, she thought he'd actually had fun. But the highlight of the whole weekend had been while the girls were at the bonfire on Saturday evening, and the long moonlit walk along the river she and Dane had shared.

Being with him, just the two of them like that, made her forget her troubles for a short time. For those brief stolen moments, nothing mattered. Would it be too much to ask for this to become her permanent home? To be a part of his life forever?

She glanced out the window at the scarecrow the girls and Dane had made. Called Mr. Scruffy, he moved around the garden as the girls saw fit. Right now, he sat in a deck chair, legs crossed, newspaper on his lap. Jodie stood behind him, arranging the patio umbrella over him to keep the rain off.

Amy shook her head.

Jodie came back inside and grinned. "I told Dad he's not allowed to burn him once we're done with him."

"Think you might lose that battle before it begins. Actually, I'm surprised he let you build one at all."

"He's a softie really."

"Your dad or Mr. Scruffy?"

Jodie laughed. "Both. Besides, Dad never liked that outfit anyway."

"No?"

"No. Not sure why."

Amy glanced at the clock. "You need to go or you'll be late for school."

Jodie nodded. "Yeah, see you tonight."

Amy watched her go, then chivied Vicky up, walking her the short distance to the primary school. She couldn't shake the feeling that she was being watched. Which was crazy because the only other people around were those either going to work, or doing the same thing she was—the school run.

She got home to find a dead cat lying in the middle of the drive. It looked like next door's. Sighing, Amy let herself in and pulled on the rubber cleaning gloves from the downstairs cloakroom. It probably died from eating all those birds and squirrels. She picked up the cat, carefully laying it on next door's lawn. Then she went inside and washed the gloves, then her hands.

First on the agenda was laundry. She had no idea

how the girls managed to make so much. Dane had finally come around to her doing his washing and left the clothes in the utility room for her. She shoved the clothes in and set the washing machine going. Next, she went to the kitchen to deal with the breakfast dishes.

She glanced out at the scarecrow. For a moment it seemed as if its head was tilted up towards the house, looking at her. She turned away and then back. The scarecrow sat studying the newspaper. Exactly the way Jodie had left it. Exactly as it should be. She must be imagining things.

Dane wouldn't let them call it a guy, not after Friday. This was probably just as well, as their creation looked nothing like a guy at all. Although after the events on the farm over the weekend, she was amazed he'd let them build one at all. There had been a fire at the farm, aside from the bonfire, and Meggie, one of the church apprentices, had been burned. Rumors abounded as to just how she'd been hurt, but Amy didn't put any store in rumors. All she knew was that was one of the cases Dane and Nate had spent so many hours working on the past few weeks.

Nate had appeared very late Saturday evening and spent an hour locked away in the study with Dane, filling him in. Maybe now that case was over, she'd see a little more of Dane.

Her thoughts returned to the scarecrow. They'd used a pumpkin for its head, Jodie carving the crookedest, not to mention ugliest, face she could manage. His body was stuffed with newspaper, and he wore Dane's old, patched jeans and a stripy jumper. Honestly, it looked like something out of a horror film, but the girls thought it was great.

Maybe she could persuade Dane to burn it at the end of the week after all. She pulled the blind. No matter how cute Jodie insisted he was, Mr. Scruffy gave her the creeps.

❧

Dane folded his arm against his chest, cradling the arm in the sling as he stood in the car park at work. He had to keep his anger in check. He glanced at Nate, and then looked back at his damaged car as another officer took photos.

"And you saw no one?" Nate asked.

"No, I didn't," Dane repeated for the umpteenth time. "I normally garage the car, but forgot to last night."

DI Welsh came down, her normally smart look slightly frazzled. "What's the damage?"

"It's been pretty badly keyed. It'll need a complete re-spray, never mind the slogan on it. Just glad Amy and the girls didn't see it. I don't want to have to explain that set of words to them."

Nate eyed the wording on the car. "I think Jodie would know what it means without you having to explain it. I know for sure that Vianne does."

Dane raised an eyebrow. "What do you teach your niece?"

"She doesn't get it from us. Actually, she tried that one out for size over the weekend. Adeline hit the roof."

"I bet she did. I imagine you did as well. What did you do? Other than ground her for the rest of her natural life."

Nate grinned. "Nah, not that long. Just until she's

thirty-two. I put a lot of soap on her toothbrush and stood over her while she cleaned her teeth. She won't be saying anything like that again for a while."

"I shall remember that one."

Welsh coughed. "If I could have your attention for just a moment, please gents. I'll get the car dusted for prints. Dane, do you have any idea who'd do this?"

"No. Assuming that we arrested the entire coven and they're not out to get me. Did you hear about the arson?"

"The one at your place? Yes, I did." His commanding officer looked even more disapproving if that were possible. "However, I would far rather have heard it from you instead than from a report dropped on my desk. But then with you two, nothing surprises me anymore. I'm arranging for a car to drive past your house four times a day." Welsh held his gaze. "Someone is targeting you—"

"Or Amy," Nate added.

"Or Miss Stabler. And for the sake of your kids, we need to do something."

"OK, fine," Dane agreed. "But it's most likely to be one of my old cases come back to haunt me. Someone with a grudge."

"That is as good a place to start as any. You and Nate get up to the office and start going through old files. Leave the car to me. I'll get someone to do it today or tomorrow. And no more driving with that shoulder until you've been cleared by the doctors. Are you sure you should be here?"

"No, Guv. Yes, Guv."

"Which is which?"

"No, I won't drive. Yes, I should be here. I'm going upstairs to sit at my desk."

"OK, make sure you do. Spend the morning with the files and then take the afternoon off. Nate, I want you to take him home no later than one."

"Will do."

Dane spent the next four hours sat at his desk, going through case after case. He sighed, tossing the file to the desk. "This is hopeless. They are all either locked up still or dead or have an alibi."

"There's got to be something," Nate reasoned. "Maybe we go further back. But tomorrow. Let's get you home."

Dane frowned. "I don't want to—"

"Ack. Guv said for you to go home at lunch. So you're going home. She already wants your guts for garters as it is. Don't make it any worse."

Dane pushed to his feet, then sat down again, as his gaze fell on the post-it-note. "Need to make a quick call first."

"Oh?"

"Amy said the gas man read the meter soon after she started working for me. I haven't had a bill yet." He dialed.

"Strange."

"Oh, yeah. I meant to chase this up last week... Yes, I'd like to inquire about my bill, please. Someone read the meter last month and nothing's arrived yet." He gave the woman his account number, tapping his pen on the desk.

The pen fell from his fingers. "Are you sure? Yes, he had ID, else we wouldn't have let him in the house. I see...No, I'll inform the police myself." He hung up and looked at Nate. "The gas man didn't come. They don't need the meter read for another three weeks."

Nate scrawled on his notepad on the desk. "I'll

chase that up with the fraud boys when I get back in. See if anyone reported any bogus callers in your area. Right now we need to get you out of here."

Dane followed Nate from the room, grabbing his coat on the way out. He gazed out the window as Nate drove, his mind running rampant. If it wasn't him, then was it Amy? OK, it was her name, and the caller had told her to "burn in hell," but could she really be the target or was it as simple as this being connected to Maranatha Farm? And if so why?

He straightened, seeing two teenage girls in school uniform running for dear life along the road in front of them. "Nate, pull over. That looks like Jodie and Vianne." As the car stopped parallel with the girls, Dane rolled down the window. "What's up?"

Jodie's wide eyes looked at him, her breath coming in rapid gasps. "Dad…"

"Where are the pair of you going so fast?"

"Home, it's a half day." She glanced over her shoulder.

"Get in. We'll take you."

"Thanks." The girls tumbled into the car.

Nate glanced over his shoulder. "Vianne, is everything OK?"

"Yes, Uncle Nate. We just got slightly creeped out by the bloke at the bus stop. Figured we'd set a new land speed record."

Dane glanced at Nate. His partner didn't seem convinced by that explanation either. He glanced back at Jodie. "What did this bloke do?"

"Just looked at us funny, that's all."

"He didn't do or say anything?"

"No, just stared at us. So we ran. We're fine, Dad."

He nodded, pulling the sunshield down and

keeping an eye on the path behind them as Nate pulled away again. It was only a couple of minutes before they reached the house. His heart dropped as he took in the red paint all over it, with Amy trying to clean it off. "What on earth is going on now?"

He got out of the car, almost before Nate had stopped it. "Amy?"

She turned, her face falling. "Oh. You're home early."

"What happened?"

"I heard something, a car maybe, and came outside and saw this. I wanted to clean it off before you came home." She looked past him, seeing the girls. "Oh."

Jodie grinned. "Half day. And it's probably a Halloween prank a little late. It happens all the time around here. Or Mr. Scruffy did it."

"Who's Mr. Scruffy?" Vianne asked.

"Come meet him. He's our scarecrow." She dashed off around the back of the house, Vianne in close pursuit.

Nate looked at Amy. "Leave it. I'll sort it. You and Dane go inside and put the kettle on."

Amy sighed. "That's just so typically English of you. We have a crisis and you want me to go and put on the kettle and make some tea."

Nate grinned. "Yes, now go. Mine's white with two sugars." He leaned into the car and pulled out the evidence bag.

Dane took Amy's hand and led her into the house. "You should have called us. We could have used some of that information. It's criminal damage for one thing. Never mind everything else that's going on." He wrinkled his nose at the smell as he passed the wet door. "That's not paint."

"No, it's fresh blood."

"Then you definitely shouldn't have cleaned it off. Has this happened before?"

Amy hesitated, before shaking her head very slightly. "Not like this, no."

"OK. Once Nate's done, I'll hose it off."

She looked behind them. "Where's your car?"

"It's gone in for repair." He shut the front door. "I scraped the paintwork."

"That was silly." She headed into the kitchen. "Can't we just wash this off and pretend none of—"

"Pretend it's not happening? No, we can't."

"Oh."

He hugged her. "No one blames you for any of this. And if you got the impression that I did, then I'm sorry. I don't."

"OK." She sucked in a deep breath. "So, Jodie says you're not burning Mr. Scruffy because he's too cute. I don't suppose there's any way that I can get you to reconsider that idea anytime soon, is there?"

"Jodie thinks she's keeping it, but she's not." He kissed her cheek then turned to put the kettle on. "Give it a week, and she'll be tired of it."

Amy glanced at the back garden where the girls were posing the scarecrow and laughed. "That's wishful thinking on your part. He's currently standing up leaning on your spade. They must have put a pole down his back."

"That's what scarecrows do."

"It's more like a scare *Amy* than a scare *crow*. He's creepy."

Dane tilted his head. "Maybe a little."

Nate came in. "Isn't that tea done yet?"

"Almost."

"Cool. OK, you can wash the front of the—" He broke off. "What in the world is that?"

Dane grinned. "Meet Mr. Scruffy."

Amy shivered. "He spent the morning sitting in a chair under an umbrella reading the paper."

Nate shook his head. "Haven't you both had enough of guys?"

"Yes," Amy said.

"This isn't a guy," Dane explained. "It's a scarecrow. And the kids wanted one. It kept them busy all yesterday afternoon."

"Rather you than me." Nate grimaced. "I wouldn't want anything that scary in my garden—besides which, Ben would probably keep knocking it over. Anyway, if you pass the hose out the cloakroom window, I'll wash the front of the house off. And then I want my tea."

Dane turned to do it, shooting off a mock salute. "Yes, Boss."

Amy laughed. "I'll do the tea, you go find the hose."

Dane followed Nate into the hall. He shut the door and lowered his voice. "I assume you took samples."

Nate nodded. "I'm taking them to the lab on my way back to work. They'll be able to tell us what sort of blood it is. I've taken photos and called it in. We can't ignore this."

"Not going to. Something is going on, and I'm not going to rest until I know what."

∼∽

Amy walked slowly through the scattered leaves

on the way to get Vicky from school. Dane had stayed at the house to keep an eye on Jodie and Vianne. They had spent the entire afternoon moving Mr. Scruffy around the garden. He was currently lying on a towel on the patio, cloud sunbathing, a book over his face. Which was definitely an improvement.

She got to the school, just as the kids came out. Vicky ran out and wrapped her arms tightly around her. Amy hugged her back. "Hey, sweetie. How are you?"

She nodded slightly. "OK," she signed.

"How's your arm?"

Vicky rubbed it. At least they'd managed to persuade her to leave the sling off now.

"Hurts, huh? But it's getting better. So let's go home and find Daddy. He might be cooking dinner."

Vicky took firm hold of her hand.

"Miss Stabler?"

Amy turned. "Miss Macnin."

"I did put a letter in Vicky's bag, but I'm trying to catch as many parents as possible. The school is closed tomorrow and Wednesday. The boiler's broken down so we have no heating or hot water."

"OK. Thank you for letting me know."

"We're hoping to be open by Thursday."

"OK." Amy looked at Vicky "So, you're off till Thursday. I think it might be time for you to teach me some more sign language."

Vicky grinned. She signed rapidly.

Amy laughed. "I have no idea what you just said, but it better not have been rude."

Vicky grinned. "Oops," she signed.

"I'll give you 'oops,'" Amy laughed.

They got back to the house to find a dead mouse

on the drive.

Vicky screwed up her nose. "Cat," she signed.

This was a bit much, especially when next door's cat was dead.

"Yes, it's like he is still giving us presents, and not very nice ones." Amy tilted her head as they walked. As usual, there was a trail of dead critters going to the door.

She let Vicky into the house, and went to find gloves to clear the mice up with. Who was being targeted here? She thought it was her, but maybe it was Dane. He certainly seemed to think so. Was someone using her to get to him? She picked up the dead critters and put them in to a carrier bag, sealing it. When she glanced up, a bloke stood opposite her watching. Then he got in to his car and drove away.

She put the bag and the gloves into the dustbin and headed inside.

Dane stood in the utility room, folding the laundry. "Are you OK, Amy?"

"Yeah, I'm fine." She wished she could be honest with him. She didn't see how he could love her once he knew the truth, and that idea terrified her. *I don't want to be alone.* She knew God loved her, despite her record, but now Rosalie was gone, she was alone.

Although, if she were honest, she lost Rosalie weeks ago when she left Filely. She let Rosalie think she was dead. The pain and grief filling her now was how Ray and Rosalie felt when she left her stuff on the beach. Maybe she should call Ray.

She looked at the phone. Slowly she picked it up and dialed.

"Hello?"

"Hello Ray. It's Amy."

"Who?"

"Amy. I just wanted to say I'm sorry about Rosalie—"

The phone went dead in her hand. The lights went out and the oven stopped working.

Dane came in. "Did the power go out?"

Amy put down the phone. "Yeah."

"I'll go check the fuses." Dane headed out.

Jodie came in. "The TV isn't working."

Amy nodded. "That's because the power has gone out."

"Cool." Jodie laughed. "Want me to go find the candles?"

"In a bit." Amy said. She looked out the window. "Where'd Mr. Scruffy go?"

"He's there."

Amy frowned. "Where? I can't see him."

"He's on the patio. You just can't see him from here."

"Well, don't keep moving him, please," Amy said, looking at her.

"It's fun," Jodie complained.

"It's creepy," Amy said.

Jodie folded her arms. "Oh, I've got no school tomorrow. It's an inset day."

"Letter?" Amy asked holding out her hand.

"No. Just kidding."

Amy rolled her eyes. "Nice try."

"I thought so. I just hope we won't be followed home or to school again."

"What do you mean?" Amy asked as her whole body grew cold.

Jodie took a deep breath. "A really creepy guy follows me everywhere. He stands outside the school at break time, too. He's been there a few days now."

Amy frowned. "Have you told anyone?"

"I just told you. And I told Dad and Uncle Nate earlier."

"Maybe I should walk you to school tomorrow."

"Please. Vianne is coming here so we can go together."

"No problem. I think Uncle Nate is taking your dad to work tomorrow anyway."

Dane came back into the kitchen. "Well it's not the fuses. Jan next door says her power is out, too. So I guess it's sandwiches for dinner."

Amy shook her head. "I can go one better than sandwiches. You have a gas hob, right?"

"Yes."

"Then give me half an hour." She looked at Jodie. "Now go put Mr. Scary back where I can see him."

"It's Scruffy not Scary." Jodie laughed.

"Whatever. Just put him back."

Jodie went outside leaving the door wide open.

Dane looked at Amy. "You do realize she will move him around the garden deliberately now, don't you?"

Something knocked on the window. Amy glanced up and jumped as Mr. Scruffy was staring right at her.

Jodie grinned waving Mr. Scruffy's arms at her. Then she put him back in the garden.

"That child will be the death of me." She groaned.

Dane grinned. "Told you." He kissed her cheek. "So I'll go find the candles while you do dinner. What are you going to do with what's in the oven?"

"I'll use it, you'll see." She busied herself with cooking.

Please let this work. It's so easy being around him.

Maybe I should tell him once this blows over, and his problems at work are sorted.

17

Amy walked Jodie and Vianne to school. She noticed they were being followed by some young guy. She looked at Jodie. "Go see Mr. Page when you get in. He'll be able to do something to stop the bloke from hanging around outside school. I'll be here at quarter past three to collect you."

Vianne looked at her. "Auntie Adeline wants me to go straight to The Dolls Hospital after school."

"I'll walk you there. That's not a problem."

"Thank you." Jodie and Vianne ran in to school.

The power was still off when Amy and Vicky got home. Workmen were digging up the road to find the source of the break. Vicky ran straight into the garden to play. Amy shook her head, watching as she pulled Mr. Scruffy off the pole and into a chair. Vicky then tugged the patio table in front of him and set the plastic princess tea set on the table.

Her mobile rang. "Hello?"

"Hi, there." Dane's voice echoed, sending ripples of pleasure through her. "How's it going?"

"We still have no power." Amy leaned against the counter. "Vicky is in the garden playing tea parties with Mr. Scruffy."

Dane chuckled. "That sounds way more fun than we're having here in the office. Is she signing to him?"

Amy watched her. "No. Her lips are moving, but I can't hear from here. I don't want to go outside and spoil the moment."

"I don't blame you. Could you do me a favor if you get chance? Pop into the hardware store and get some phone cable and tacks?"

"Is that the one along the High Street?"

"Yeah. I won't get there before it shuts tonight."

Amy hesitated. "If I can, yeah."

"Thank you. That way I can move the phone from the study into the lounge. What's that noise in the background?"

Amy wandered through to the lounge. "The workmen are digging up the road trying to find out why there is no power." She watched the men working for a while from behind the net curtains. "Although I have never seen a foreman without a yellow jacket or a hard helmet before."

"Stop ogling the workmen."

Amy laughed. "Not jealous are you?"

"Yes. Now go do some hoovering."

"There's no power."

"Fine. Do some laundry then."

"Uh, there's no power."

"Watch TV then."

Amy screamed with laughter. "Which part of 'there's no power' don't you understand?"

Dane chuckled. "It's the combination of the three words that's confusing me. Well as there's no power, I suggest you better go to bed and eat cream cakes then."

"That sounds perfect."

"Or not, because you can't wash the sheets when you get crumbs all over them."

"Go do some work. I'll see you tonight." Amy hung up and went outside to check on Vicky.

❧❧

Dane sat at his desk having gone through all of his back cases. "Did you hear back about the gas man?"

"There were three other bogus calls in your road on the same day. But nothing since. We're working on getting descriptions, but it was a while ago now. Problem is people remember the uniform and not the faces behind them."

"Yeah." He tossed the last file to the desk. "Nothing." He sighed.

Nate glanced up. "There must be one you've overlooked."

"There isn't." Dane rubbed his shoulder. On a scale of one to ten, the pain was probably a seven right now.

"Then maybe we should check out Amy after all."

Dane looked at him.

"Mate, I know how you feel about her, and believe me I'm not saying this to be mean, or to try and break the two of you up."

"Yeah, right."

"I mean you love her unconditionally, right? And so long as she is not on the sex-offenders list, you have no problem with her being around your kids, right?"

Dane nodded.

"Then there is no harm in looking, is there? If it's not you, what else could it be?"

Dane yawned. "Tomorrow. Right now, it's late and I'm tired."

Nate looked at him. "That's not like you."

Dane shrugged and regretted it. He rubbed his shoulder and winced. "Yeah, well." He followed Nate from the room to the stairs.

DI Welsh caught them up as they reached the stairwell. "I have had a call from Liam Page. He is head of English at Headley Cross Secondary. A few of the kids have reported a man hanging around the school gates. I'm putting uniform there tomorrow, but wanted you to both know as you have girls there."

"Thank you." Dane looked at Nate. "Maybe we should go through your cases, too."

Nate nodded. "Tomorrow. I assume there is CCTV footage for us to look at, Guv?"

"It will be on your desk first thing in the morning."

"Thank you." Dane walked with Nate, who was chatting on the phone to Adeline.

Nate hung up. "Vianne is at The Dolls Hospital. Amy dropped her off after school. Vianne said she has seen this bloke on and off for the past week or so. I'll talk to her when I get in."

Dane got into the car. "This whole thing is making me more than a little uncomfortable."

Nate started the car. "So, we've got a bloke hanging around the school—most likely the one the girls were running from yesterday. Blood on your front door, criminal damage to your car, and lots of nasty calls to your house—all directed at Amy."

"Don't forget the gas man that wasn't. And the arson."

"And Amy's friend being kidnapped and murdered." Nate glanced at him. "That's way too much to be a coincidence."

Dane nodded. "If it were anyone else we'd have acted way before now."

"Yeah. We'll look into my cases tomorrow, but

honestly, we need to run at least a cursory background check on Amy. If not a more detailed one." Nate pulled up outside the house. "Is your power still off?"

Dane looked up at the dark house. "It looks that way. Either that or the girls have convinced Amy to do a candlelit dinner again."

"You want to come and stay with us?"

He shook his head. "Nah, we'll be fine. It's like camping. The only difference being it's indoors and we don't get wet or blown away. I'll see you tomorrow."

He let himself into the house. "Hello?"

"In the kitchen," Amy called.

He went in. The gas lamp glowed on the bench and the girls sat crouched around it doing homework. Amy stood by the hob, stirring something that smelled delicious.

Dane kissed the girls' heads, and then crossed over to Amy. "How have they been?"

"Fine."

"We are bored of the dark," Jodie said.

"You are, are you?" Dane laughed. "I thought you liked candlelit meals."

"Once in a blue moon, not three times a day. We want the lights and the TV back again. And don't think we can't see you hugging Amy from here, because we can."

"I wasn't," Dane protested.

"Then why weren't you hugging her?" Jodie looked at him. "We know you like her, Dad. It's obvious."

Vicky nodded.

"It is, is it?" Dane asked.

"Yes. So by all means hug her, but don't do any of that kissy-kissy stuff, because that's disgusting."

Amy laughed.

Dane hugged her. "There, everyone happy now?"

"Yes," Jodie said. "Dad, when are they fixing the lights?"

"Hopefully tomorrow. Jodie, we had a phone call from the school, from your English teacher."

"Yeah. Mr. Page said he'd ring. Vianne and I went to see him at break. He's been hanging around for a while."

"I assume you mean the bloke you were running from yesterday, and not Mr. Page?"

She looked at him for a moment, and then nodded. "Yeah. He didn't do anything; it's just a little creepy having him hanging out there watching us."

"Could you describe the bloke for me?"

"Sure. But we can go one better than that, can't we, Amy?"

Amy pulled out her phone. "Sure can. I got the girls to pose outside the school gates before we left. The bloke you want is in the background."

Dane hugged her and kissed her. "Amy, you're brilliant."

"I said *don't* kiss her," Jodie complained. "Ewww. That's gross."

Vicky grinned, signing the same thing.

Dane scowled.

Amy ignored her. "I do my best to be brilliant," she said.

"Text it to me, please. I'll forward it to Nate and my DI."

Amy did so, and then turned off her phone. "The battery's low. Need to keep what little charge there is for the school run tomorrow."

Dane looked at the photo on his phone. First thing

in the morning he was going to run a background check on Amy.

Nate was right. If it wasn't either of them, then it had to be her.

ᚷᚫᚷ

Dane sat in front of the computer and scowled at it, almost as hard as he had frowned at his phone earlier that morning. Everything seemed to be conspiring against him.

"What's up now?" Nate asked as he trawled through mug shots, trying to place their mystery school gate stalker. The police presence had at least scared him off for the time being.

"Either I'm not looking right, or there's something wrong with the system."

Nate scooted his chair across the carpet. "Why?"

"There is no record anywhere of an Amy Stabler." Not born the year she claims she was anyway. Nor is there an on-line presence either."

Nate tilted his head. "You're not on a certain social media site either."

"I have my reasons."

"Amy must exist," Nate said. "She's at home with Vicky."

"And Jodie." Dane pulled out his phone and showed him the text. "The school has no power so they sent everyone home. I guess the power outage is spreading."

"Where's Vianne?"

"Amy dropped her off at the Doll hospital with Adeline. But by all means, feel free to double-check."

"I will." Nate pulled out his phone and dialed.

"Maybe she lied about her birthday. You know how some women are with their ages."

Dane tuned him out. There was nothing, and there should at least be something. He pulled up the main database. He didn't want to do this, but he had no choice. Slowly he typed Amy's name into the national database.

Nothing.

He leaned back in his chair, his hands falling to his lap. Stunned shock filled him.

"Dane?" Nate touched his arm. "What is it?"

"She doesn't exist," he said numbly. "No national insurance, no school records, banks, or anything. So who's at home looking after my daughters?"

Nate picked up the phone. "I'll call Ray Malone. She claims to know him, right?"

"Yeah."

"So we ask him. I'll put it on speaker so you can hear what he has to say. I'll call his mobile rather than the landline."

"Oh?"

Nate just looked at him. "When Jas died, you ignored the landline for weeks. You'd only answer your mobile because you knew it wasn't going to be a reporter."

"Good point."

❦

Amy carried the lunch dishes into the kitchen. They'd had a picnic in the study and now the girls were in the lounge. She grinned as Jodie jumped up in front of the kitchen window and pulled faces at her. Amy pulled one back and headed to the study for the rest of the dishes.

She brought them into the kitchen and put them by the sink. Turning on the taps, she squirted washing up liquid in and then picked up a plate. She glanced up and jumped, crying out in fright.

Mr. Scruffy filled the kitchen window. His twig hands rested on the glass, either side of his evil grinning pumpkin head. The plate fell from her hand and smashed on the tiled floor.

She sucked in a deep breath, turning her back on him, shaking hard. She stood there for a moment, before bending to pick up the pieces of broken china. "Jodie, that isn't funny anymore," she yelled.

Jodie appeared in the doorway leading to the hall. "What isn't funny anymore? Oh, you broke a plate."

Amy looked up. "Moving Mr. Scruffy isn't funny. And leaning him against the kitchen window like that definitely isn't. He scared me half to death."

Jodie frowned. "I didn't put him there."

Amy raised her hands impersonating the scarecrow, right down to his evil grinning face. "He was like that, peering through the window when I came in with the dishes."

"But I didn't do it. And he isn't there now, look."

Amy looked over at the window. He wasn't there. "He's gone."

Jodie grinned. "I reckon you're seeing things."

She shook her head. "I'm not seeing things. I'm telling you he was right against the window."

"Then where is he?" Jodie pulled herself up onto the counter and peered through the glass. "I can't see him."

"Get down before you fall and end up in a sling, too. I have enough one-armed bandits in the house as it is."

"OK." Jodie turned and prepared to jump down. Her eyes widened, color drained from her face and she screamed.

Amy dropped the cup into the sink. "Now what?"

Jodie pointed behind her, still screaming.

Amy turned.

Mr. Scruffy stood right behind them, wind blowing through the open door, as he reached for her.

18

Dane sat, lacing his fingers and unlacing them, worry gnawing at his gut. Had he made a mistake hiring Amy? Had he made an even bigger mistake in falling for her? Had he let her bedazzle him and use her good looks to lure him into a false sense of security?

Nate hit the speaker button as the phone was answered. "Hello, Ray, it's Nate Holmes from Headley Cross. How are you?"

"Not so bad." Even to Dane, Pastor Malone sounded depressed. He knew what it was like to lose your wife in such ugly circumstances.

"I'm really sorry to hear about Rosalie. How are you really doing?"

"It's hard, but God's giving me the grace to get through each day, albeit barely. And I have Sara. How are you and your family?"

"We're doing OK. I'm sorry to bother you at a time like this, but I need your help."

"If I can. What do you need?"

Nate looked over at Dane. "We're trying to trace a woman called Amy Stabler. All our normal avenues of investigation have turned up nothing. She claims to know you and your wife. Actually, she said she was your wife's best friend. According to Amy, she and Rosalie went to university together, roomed together whilst there, and when you and your wife married and moved to Filely, she moved with you, renting her own place not far from the manse. She was pretty upset when your wife died."

"I'm sorry. Amy—who did you say?"

"Stabler. She's twenty-seven. She has hazel eyes, long wavy red hair. She's very pretty. Good with kids. She said she worked in the church crèche. I'm assuming that would be your church."

"I'm afraid I can't help you. At least not in the way you'd like me to." There was a long pause. "Amy's dead."

"I'm sorry?"

"Amy is dead. I never knew the woman you've just described, at least not by that name. Rosie's best friend was Amy Childs. But she was blonde, although she always wanted red hair. She died several weeks ago. She was washed out to sea, they never found her body. Rosie was devastated. But Amy had been really down after the accident and the trial. We couldn't help but wonder if it really was an accidental drowning or if she'd intended it."

Dane frowned. "What trial?"

Nate looked at him. "Ray, I have you on speaker phone so my partner can hear you. His name is DS Philips. What trial?"

Dane's stomach turned, and he swallowed the rising nausea. Whom had he employed? *God, please overrule with this mess I have made. Help me put it right. Keep my kids safe.*

Pastor Malone spoke again. "Amy did a U-turn, and hit a pedestrian. He wasn't badly hurt, but the police got involved. She was arrested and charged with careless driving. She pleaded guilty and got a twelve month suspended sentence and a huge fine, which she paid. And she lost her license for a year as well. But it didn't end there. There were a couple of fires at her place, death threats, silent phone calls, someone tried to kill her as well. Then she left her stuff on the beach and walked into the sea. Her body was never found."

Dane and Nate exchanged horrified glances. Dane turned to the computer and typed Amy Childs into the database. He got an instant match. It was her. *His* Amy. The woman he'd put in charge of his kids and had fallen in love with, had some maniac trying to kill her. No wonder stuff was happening. No wonder she'd been so cagy about her past and hadn't wanted to drive when he asked her to.

He shook his head. "She's broken her sentencing conditions," he said quietly. He'd have to arrest her the next time he saw her. "Nate." He turned the screen so his partner could see it. "It's her."

Nate's eyes widened. "Ray, Amy's alive. She's right here in Headley Cross."

"You're kidding."

"No. Your Amy Childs is our Amy Stabler."

Dane read slowly. "It sounds like someone big was after her." He caught his breath. *Lord God, it can't be. Surely I'm reading this wrong.* "Nate..."

Nate looked over as he finished the call and hung up. "What is it?"

"The guy she ran over. It was Derek Saunders."

Nate paled. "The guy we met in Filely?"

"Yes. *Kevin* Saunders's brother." He pushed upright. "I need to get home now."

"I'll take you."

DI Welsh came in. Did that woman know instantly he left his desk? "Where are you two off to now?"

"Following up a new line of investigation." Not

bothering to explain, Dane put his coat on as he pulled his mobile from his pocket. He dialed Amy's mobile and headed to the door as he waited for her to pick up. The panic inside him grew exponentially as the phone rang off the hook. "There's no answer. I have to get over there. Nate, we gotta run."

Nate shot their boss an apologetic look as he hurtled from the room after Dane.

क्ष्प्र

Amy scooted backwards, trying to protect Jodie as Mr. Scruffy moved towards them.

"How is that possible?" Jodie shrieked.

"I don't know."

Mr. Scruffy reached for Amy and she dodged, sending the vase of flowers crashing to the floor. She grabbed Jodie's hand and ran for the door, sliding on the wet tiles.

Three men wearing masks appeared in the doorway with guns.

Jodie screamed as one man grabbed her, pulling her away from Amy.

Amy reached for her, her feet slipping. "Leave her alone!"

Another grabbed Amy. "No, you don't. You're not going anywhere."

The third man came over to her. "It's so nice to see you again, Amy." He looked over at Mr. Scruffy. "Search the house, and then burn it. The rest of you put these two in the car."

Amy struggled as they dragged her and Jodie out of the house. *God keep Vicky safe in there. And protect us.* "You don't need Jodie," she yelled. "Let her go."

"Shut up." A blow jolted her head sideways, and she saw stars. To her left she saw Jodie struggle before she was picked up and tossed in the car. Someone shoved her sideways and she fell into the vehicle, hitting her head on the metal frame as she did.

The door slammed shut. She felt for a handle, but there was none.

"Where's Vicky?" Jodie signed frantically as the car moved.

"In the house," Amy whispered. She turned and looked.

Flames leapt from the study window. *Please God, look after Vicky, and get her out of there.*

❧

Dane prayed hard as Nate sped along the streets from the police station to his house. His body taut as a violin bow, he had a horrid feeling they'd run out of time. It was like that awful night when Nate had turned up on his doorstep to tell him that Jas was dead.

Two patrol cars also turned into his road, one in front of them, one behind, blues and twos echoing. The bad feeling grew. They hadn't told anyone. What else was happening for uniform to turn up in such numbers?

They rounded the corner to find flames shooting from the study and lapping up the side of the house.

His heart sank and then stopped. His kids were in there. "Noooo…"

Nate skidded the car to a halt, stopping it on the handbrake.

Dane leapt from the car and ran towards the house, screaming at the top of his voice. "Jodie! Vicky!

Amy!" He hurtled up the path and shouldered the door. It didn't give. He pulled out his key, fumbling with it. Something in the study exploded, sending sparks and flames shooting through the window.

Sirens blared from somewhere behind him as he pushed open the door. Thick black smoke billowed out.

"Dane, wait," Nate yelled.

Dane ignored him, plunging into the burning building, desperate to find his daughters and pull them out. The thick smoke choked him, the flames crackled, heat blasting from the study door. "Vicky? Jodie? Amy?"

God, please a little help here. Let me find them.

He looked in the lounge and kitchen, but there was no one there. Putting a hand over his mouth, he fought his way through the smoke up the stairs. Amy's room, above the study, was ablaze.

He pushed open Vicky's door. "Vicky! Jodie! Are you in here?"

A whimper came from the wardrobe, barely audible over the noise of the fire.

He ran over to it, coughing, and flung open the door.

Vicky sat curled up at the bottom of the wardrobe, clutching her teddy, tears falling down her cheeks. Her whole body shook, and she rocked slowly back and forth.

Thank You.

"I got you," he whispered. He pushed his arm out of the sling, and gathered her into his arms. He grunted as pain shot through him. The grunt turned to a muffled scream as he stood, holding Vicky tightly to his chest.

Her arm snaked around his neck, her tears soaking his collar.

"It's OK," he managed. He took one step, almost losing his balance.

God, help me get out Vicky of here, please. Don't let me drop her.

Two fire fighters in full kit appeared behind him. "Let's get you out of here." The voice was familiar, but he couldn't place it in all the confusion around him.

"I have to find the others."

"We'll do that. Right now I want you and Vicky out of here." One of them led him into his room where a ladder rested against the window.

Tears tracked down his face as they took Vicky from him, handing her out of the window.

"Now you," the fire fighter said.

He looked at him, suddenly recognizing the eyes. "Jared?"

Jared Harkin, friend and fellow church member nodded. "Now, out, so I can do my job. Who's still missing?"

"Jodie has to be in here somewhere. And Amy. She was looking after the girls while I was at work." He slowly slid outside, letting the other firefighter guide him down the ladder.

Nate stood at the bottom. "Idiot," he hissed. "There's being a hero and being stupid."

"Where's Vicky?"

"Right here." The voice belonged to another firefighter.

"I couldn't find them. Only Vicky. Vicky, sweetie..."

She scrambled into his arms.

"I couldn't find them." Dane repeated.

"Not there," Vicky whispered.

He looked at her. Was he hearing things? "Sweetie?"

"Mr. Scruffy took them," she whispered.

"Honey, Mr. Scruffy is a scarecrow. He can't move."

Nate put a hand on his arm. "Dane, she's terrified, but she's talking. Just let her say what she saw, we'll make sense of it later. Go on, Vicky. What did Mr. Scruffy do?"

"Chased them, took them away." Tears ran unchecked down her face.

"I don't understand," Dane said.

"Mr. Scruffy took them," she whispered. "Put them in a car."

Dane looked at Nate. Vicky had no reason to lie, even if she was confusing the scarecrow with someone else. "Tell the firefighters they're not in the house."

DI Welsh ran over to them. "Is everyone out?"

Dane looked at her. "He's got Jodie and Amy."

"Who has?"

"It has to be Saunders. Her real name is Amy Childs. She hit Derek Saunders with her car, and got done for careless driving. She fled here in fear of her life. Only he found her and now he has Jodie."

A paramedic came over, trying to take Vicky.

Dane held her tightly.

DI Welsh put a hand on his arm. "Dane, you need to let them check her over, make sure she's OK."

"I need to keep her safe. But I also need to find Jodie." He looked at Vicky, torn as to what to do. Why was this so hard?

Nate nodded, pulling out his phone. "And we will, but you and Vicky need to be checked over first.

I'll get Adeline to come over and collect Vicky. She'll be safe at ours."

Vicky clung to him tightly. "Stay with Daddy," she whispered.

Dane hugged her. "Honey, I know you want to and I want that more than anything, but I have to go and find Jodie and I need you to be safe. Auntie Adeline will keep you safe."

"Mr. Scruffy took them."

"Mr. Scruffy is a scarecrow."

"He was in the house. We didn't always move him. He did it himself."

"Mr. Scruffy was in the house?" Dane shook his head, trying to understand what she was saying. "Where were you?"

"In my kitchen den. Then I hid in my room. He hurt her. He twisted Jodie's arm and he hit Amy."

Anger flooded him. "And I'll hurt him when I find him."

"Dane," Nate warned.

"Fine." He looked at the paramedic. "You can check her over, but she's not moving from here." He gazed up at the house, the study and Amy's room well alight. So much for his safe refuge.

Vicky snuggled against him as the paramedic checked her over. He didn't let go, thrilled by the fact she'd spoken. He just wished her first words had been something other than this. The irony hit him hard. She'd stopped talking when her mother died, and started again when her sister vanished.

Adeline arrived. "Hi. Is everyone all right?"

"No," he said quietly.

Nate quickly filled his wife in, using a combination of speech and sign.

The paramedic looked at Dane. "She's fine. She just needs to be kept warm."

"Thanks."

Vicky waved to him, and then clung to her father again.

Dane glanced over to see Vianne in the car, her face pressed against the glass, fear in her eyes. He looked at Vicky. "Sweetie, go with Auntie Adeline and Ben."

She shook her head. "Stay with Daddy," she whispered.

Adeline knelt next to her. "You'll be safe with me. Daddy and Uncle Nate need to find Jodie and Amy."

Vicky cried, holding tightly to Dane.

Tears filled his eyes. *What do I do? Leave them or leave her?* He kissed Vicky's forehead. "Vicks, I promise I'll be back. But I need you safe and you can't stay here with the house on fire, because it's not safe. Auntie Adeline and Vianne will look after you."

Adeline took her hand. "We'll go via the chip shop," she said. "Would you like that? Or would you prefer pizza or burger?"

"Pizza," she whispered.

At that, Dane really did choke up. The first meal she'd asked for in years and it was Jas's favorite.

Adeline smiled. "Then we'll go to my house and you and Vianne can look at the delivery menu and order whatever you like."

Vicky nodded slowly. She looked at Dane. "Are you coming?"

"I will be, just as soon as I find Jodie and Amy." He hugged her. "Be good I love you."

Vicky hugged him tightly. "Love you, Daddy."

He closed his eyes, tears running down his face as

he held her tightly. He'd waited so long to hear those words, and he'd about given up hope.

Nate put a hand on his shoulder. "It's time to let her go, mate. There'll be a marked car outside my place, and an officer in the house, until we find the others."

"OK." He kissed Vicky and slowly let go of her.

Vicky stood and took Adeline's hand. "Bye Daddy."

"Bye, sweetie. See you soon."

Adeline left, flanked by a police officer. Dane kept an eye on her as she led Vicky to the car and strapped her in. He raised a hand and waved slightly as the car pulled away, escorted by a patrol car.

Only when the car was out of sight, did he look at Nate. "Where do we start?"

DI Welsh coughed. He'd forgotten she was there. "You're not going to start anything."

Dane scowled. "That's my daughter out there."

"That's exactly why you're not getting involved. Let us handle it."

Dane looked at his house. The fire seemed confined to one side. He had no idea where they'd sleep tonight, but honestly, he didn't care. He'd sleep in the car once he knew Jodie and Amy were safe.

Jared crossed over to him. "Dane?"

"Jared. How is it?"

"Under control, but we'll be here a while yet. I don't need to tell you it was arson. The study and bedroom above are going to be a total loss. The rest should be OK apart from some smoke damage. We'll get the structural engineers in once we've finished as you can't go back in until it's been declared safe."

"Thank you."

❧

Dane sat in his office and pulled up every scrap of information he could find on the Saunders brothers. The drugs he already knew about. It was everything else he needed to know. And he didn't like what was coming up on his screen.

Nate put a mug of coffee on his desk. "Anything?"

"Thanks, mate." Dane picked up the cup. "Saunders runs Filely by the looks of it—and more than just in his capacity as mayor. The rumors were true. He took Mrs. Malone and killed her to get to Amy. But I still don't understand how he found Amy when she'd left no trace at all. She did a perfect vanishing job. Much better than anything I'd have done. She asked to be paid in cash. I therefore didn't need her bank details. She must have gotten fake ID from somewhere."

"Not necessarily. You don't need ID for a library card or a bus pass."

"You should read this." DI Welsh dropped a report on his desk. "How are you doing?"

"I'm just fine." Dane flicked through the file. Dead animals, blood covering the windows on more than one occasion... How had he not known all this was going on at his own house? Was he so blinded by his feelings for Amy that nothing else mattered?

He looked up. "I don't understand why any of this is happening. OK, Amy broke the law, but she pleaded guilty, the court punished her. That should have been the end of it. Why is this guy hounding her? Surely he must know his position as mayor is over when he gets caught."

DI Welsh sat on the edge of his desk. "Apparently the wrong judge got the case. It should have been Judge Paul, who it turns out, is on Kevin Saunders' pay roll, but she was sick. She's now been arrested herself. Rather than put off the case as it was a simple sentencing, Judge Barrowman did it. Saunders thought the sentence too light."

Dane groaned. "And Amy's broken the conditions of her suspended sentence. I find her and I'm going to have to arrest her before she can count to three." He sucked in a deep breath and rubbed his hand over his face, his shoulder hurting again. "Hi, Amy. We came to rescue you. By the way, now we've done that, I'm afraid you're under arrest for breaking your sentencing conditions."

Nate looked at him. "What?"

"She lost her license. A twelve month driving ban and I made her drive me and Vicky to the hospital."

DI Welsh shook her head. "Don't worry about that now. And don't arrest her the next time you see her. I'll deal with it once she's back safely. But let's just find her and Jodie, and get them home safe first, before we worry about anything else."

"He wants her dead." Dane pushed his hand through his hair. "Like he killed Rosalie Malone."

"Not going to happen," Nate said firmly.

DI Welsh agreed. She glanced around the office and, seeing it was empty, lowered her voice. "Just between us, Mrs. Malone isn't dead."

Nate frowned. "She's what?"

"She's badly injured and under heavy guard at Headley General. I had her moved here under a false name when they found her at the bottom of the cliff. She's officially 'dead' until the situation in Filely is under control. Maybe permanently in the WPS; that's dependent on what the CPS decide to do. 'Need to know' only, which you two do."

"Does her husband know?"

"He and the baby are staying at the hospital, again under armed guard for now."

"So when I spoke to him, he was up the road."

DI Welsh nodded. "But like I said, need to know. As far as the Filely plod is concerned, she's dead." The door opened and another officer came in. She raised her voice to a normal level. "We've got the number and make of the car. The roads between here and Filely are being watched. He won't get far."

Nate nodded. "I mean, how many cars do you see being driven by pumpkin headed scarecrows anyway?"

DI Welsh rolled her eyes. "I'm sorry?"

"According to Vicky, Mr. Scruffy did it. He broke into the house and took Jodie and Amy away." He stopped, grabbing the report. *"Half the time the scarecrow moved without the girls being outside,"* he read.

Dane froze. "He's been out there the whole time, watching her. I just gave him the access he needed."

❧

Amy sat in the tiny room in the flat, her hands tied behind her back. Jodie sat next to her, similarly tied up. She looked at her. "Jodie, are you all right?"

"Peachy," Jodie replied. "What about you? You banged your head pretty hard. It's bleeding."

"It hurts," Amy admitted. "But what matters is getting out of here."

"How?"

"I don't know, but God will find a way."

"Is this all part of His plan too?" Jodie scoffed. "Getting hit and kidnapped and having my sister die in a fire?"

"I'm sure Vicky got out, because the neighbors would have called the fire brigade and they'd come really, really fast. And no, this isn't part of God's plan for us. But it happened and He'll help us get through it." She paused. "It's because we live in a sin-filled world, evil just messes things up sometimes."

"Like when Mum died? That was an act of evil rather than God being mean to me."

Amy nodded, despite the pain in her face. "You got it. Evil breaks in, messes things up, then God turns on the light and shows us a way through it."

The door opened and Derek Saunders came in. "Amy, it's so nice to bump into you again."

"What do you want?" Amy asked.

"Revenge. See, the courts didn't do it properly. You were meant to go down. It was arranged, and once inside, there would be a welcoming committee for you."

Amy swallowed hard.

Jodie frowned. "I don't understand. Go down where?"

"Didn't she tell you what she'd done or who she really is? She's a criminal with a record. She mowed me down like an innocent daisy in a field of long grass."

Jodie laughed. "You're a daisy? More like a dandelion."

"Shut up." Derek scowled at her. "You're just collateral damage. Like the pastor's wife."

Amy gasped. "You killed Rosalie?"

"She insisted you were dead, but we knew better. It'd had taken us some time but we finally tracked you by the fake ID you ordered on the internet. Mrs. Malone was, shall we say, payback part one."

Jodie looked at her. "Your name isn't Amy?"

Amy shook her head. "My name *is* Amy, just not Amy Stabler. It's Amy Childs. Everything else I told you is the truth. I had to run away and change my name because this man wanted me dead. I'm sorry. All this is my fault."

"Yes, it is. All your fault." Derek put a gun to Amy's head. "And now I'm going to kill you the same way you almost killed me. But first…payback part two. Well, three, if you include the child we burned in the house." He swung the gun around and aimed at Jodie.

Jodie screamed.

Amy swallowed down her terror. She knew what she had to do. It might not work, but she had to try. "Let Jodie go. And you can do what you want with me. You said she's collateral, means nothing. So let her go and keep me. I have money. You can have that in exchange for her."

"You're selling me?" Jodie managed.

"Buying your freedom," Amy told her. She looked back at Derek. "Keep me, just let her go."

"How much?"

"I have twenty thousand. It's in cash. Just let me or Jodie call her father. He can bring the cash wherever you want."

"Assuming it didn't burn."

"It wasn't in the house. It's in the boot of Dane's car. In a tin."

Derek nodded. He handed Jodie the phone. "You tell him exactly what I write down. Don't you go telling him nothing else. And be quick about it. I don't want them tracing the call."

"OK."

He wrote quickly then held the paper out to her. "Here."

Jodie looked at Amy.

She nodded. "It's for the best. Just do it."

Jodie nodded and dialed slowly. "I just hope his phone is switched on."

"It will be," Amy said. *It has to be.*

19

Dane sat at his desk, fuming. His fingers drummed on the desk over and over. "It's my lead."

DI Welsh looked at him. "You're staying put."

"But Guv…"

She shook her head firmly. "But nothing. As far as this case goes, you're *the victim,* not the investigating officer."

He turned to his partner. "Nate?"

"Nothing I can do."

Dane shot Nate a withering look. "Thanks for the backup. Can I remind you who charged into a building filled with active gunfire to help you save Adeline? Aside from the armed MI5 officer, that is."

Nate held up his hands. "I know. But it's not my call."

Dane looked back at his boss. "So you're not going to humor me and let me go anyway."

She narrowed her eyes. "No. Nate will follow it up. I suggest you go and find Vicky and be with her. Nate, I need to speak to you in my office."

"Yes, Guv." Nate shot Dane a compassionate look before following her from the room.

"Go home," Dane muttered. "And how am I meant to do that when my home is on fire, cordoned off and she told me not to drive?" His phone rang, and he pulled it out. "Philips."

"Daddy…"

"Jodie?" He sat bolt upright in his chair. "Where are you?"

"A man has me and Amy. He says I can come home if you bring him twenty thousand pounds. It's in a tin in the boot of your car. Amy says the money is hers, but she insists you use it. The man says to bring all the money to the park at quarter to six tonight by the war memorial. He says to come alone and not be late, and he'll let me go."

Dane glanced at the clock on the wall. It was four-thirty. Hopefully his car was finished. It was at the garage across the road being resprayed. "What about Amy?"

"He said just me. If you come with anyone, he'll kill me. I love you, Daddy." The phone went dead.

"Jodie?" Dane buried his head in his hands. *God, please, I don't often ask for a miracle, but I really need one about now.*

Nate came over to him. "Dane? Who was on the phone?"

Dane stood and ignored the question. He wasn't going to lose Jodie and Amy like he'd lost Jasmine. "Is my car ready?"

"Yes, the garage brought it back twenty minutes ago, but you can't drive one-handed."

"It's a semi-automatic, so yes I can. I don't usually use it as such, but today I will."

"Where are you going?"

"Home," he snapped. "See what's left of it, then go and pick Vicky up. Find somewhere to stay."

"You're staying with us. That goes without saying. The Guv wants a word."

"I have to go. I'll speak to her tomorrow." He strode to the door, leaving Nate standing there. He didn't have a choice. He had to go alone.

As he ran down the hallway, a verse from Matthew echoed through his mind. *"I am with you always, even unto the end of the world."*

He wasn't going alone. He just prayed he'd be in time and be able to save them both.

➶◈

Derek snatched the phone from Jodie and turned it off. "Get over there."

Jodie scooted back to Amy and leaned against her. "I'm scared."

Amy nodded. "Me too, but it'll be all right."

"Did you really hit that man with your car?"

Amy swallowed hard. She hadn't wanted the truth to come out like this. "Yes, but I didn't mean to. It was an accident. I did a U-turn, because I was running late for a party, and he was in the way."

"In the way?" Derek yelled. "I was not in the way. *You* mounted the pavement and *you* hit me. You shouldn't have been there. People don't treat the Saunders brothers like that and get away with it."

"It wasn't deliberate. I pled guilty, paid my fine. You tried to kill me. Even drove me out of town."

"You ran. Faked your own death, like the coward you are."

Jodie looked up. "She's not a coward. She's one of the bravest people I know."

"I'm sorry," Amy said again. She didn't care what happened to her. So long as Jodie was safe.

Her thoughts turned to Vicky. Had she gotten out of the blazing house? Or had Amy failed her, too?

"So we meet again." Polished boots appeared in

her field of vision.

She jerked her head up, passed pressed slacks, shirt, tie, and jacket, to the scarred face she knew from before. "It's you—"

Kevin Saunders nodded. "Yes, it's me. I wanted justice to be done as it should have been. And that didn't happen. You cheated the system. But no one can run from me for long." He ran his fingers down her face, and she pulled away. "You see, Amy, you need to pay for what you did. You were clever to fake your own death, but not clever enough for me."

"What are you going to do?"

"Kill you."

She looked at him with every ounce of defiance she could manage. "And Jodie? What about her?"

"She can go once I get the money you promised." His fingers raked her skin. "So noble."

"Her life comes before mine, every single time."

"Like my brother's before mine. I think we finally understand each other. Very well. You may exchange your life for hers."

෯෯

Dane drove from the work car park to the nearest layby. Jumping out he ran around to the boot, hoping the tin was there. He couldn't have searched for it at work. That would have been too obvious. Besides, he didn't want Nate or the Guv coming out to find him searching the car. *God, can I have a little help, please?*

Sure enough in the boot of his car was a tin containing Amy's money. She'd hidden it well. He'd never have found it if he hadn't been looking for it. He didn't want to know what she was doing with that much money. Was that why they'd taken her? She'd lied to him. He'd known something was wrong, and she hadn't come to him.

Of course he knew why now. She was a convicted criminal. He was a cop. Or should that be Cop with a capital C. Someone she couldn't trust. There was no way he could have a relationship with her or any woman if trust wasn't there.

But he still wanted it.

He wanted her.

After all, if he turned it into an analogy, a sinner was simply another word for a criminal, wasn't it? And they were all sinners in God's eyes. And no one was worthy, but all could be forgiven, no matter what they had done.

He drove through the dark streets to the park. Once the clocks changed, the nights drew in earlier and earlier. He parked and looked at the tin. If he'd had time, or thought about it beforehand, he'd have picked up a case with a tracker in it and transferred all the money to that. But it was too late. Then he locked the car and walked to the base of the war memorial.

Lord, please let him turn up. Let him free Jodie and Amy. I might have to negotiate for Amy, but I love her. It doesn't matter what she did, we can work this out. Just give us the chance to do so. Please...

A second car pulled up to the war memorial. A man got out. Dane caught a brief glimpse of Amy in the car. The man opened the door and yanked out Jodie, a gun pressed against her head. Another man pulled out Amy.

Nausea and rage filled him. Terror knotted his gut, and his tie threatened to choke him. That was his little girl in danger. It was all he could do not to charge over there. That would only get Jodie or Amy hurt or killed. He stood slowly.

"Daddy…" Jodie's cry was cut short, and his anger rose.

One of the men shoved Amy towards him.

She stumbled, almost falling before regaining her balance. She slowly walked over to him. "Have you got the money?"

"Yes."

She held out a hand.

"Amy, we can work this out."

"Just give me the money, please, Dane."

"Why?"

"Because if you don't, then they'll kill Jodie, like they killed Rosalie. Because of me. I'm buying her freedom with this."

"What about you?" His throat constricted. He could still lose them both.

"I'm beyond redemption. She's a good kid, a brave one. Look after her."

Dane gave her the tin, the pad of his thumb running over her fingers. "I will. It's all there."

Amy held his gaze. "Is Vicky…? Did she get out of the house?"

"Yeah, she's fine, I got her out. She actually spoke, told me who'd taken you."

Tears tracked slowly down Amy's face. "I'm glad."

"Amy…" He reached out for her, grabbing her arm. "Rosalie isn't dead."

"What?" She looked at him, and then shook her head. "Don't…it's not fair."

"I promise, she's safe. The report was a false one to protect her. Let me help you, now."

"I can't." She turned to go.

"Amy…"

"Please, Dane," her voice trembled, the emotion in it causing his heart to swell and threaten to break. "Don't make this any harder for me that it already is."

"I love you."

She turned, a haunted look in her tear-filled eyes. "I love you, too. Bye."

Dane's hand fell to his side as she moved away and headed back to the car. He didn't want to let her go, but his daughter's life was at stake. Once Jodie was safe, he'd come back for Amy. He wasn't going to leave her to die here.

The man holding Jodie pushed her away so hard she almost fell.

Dane held out a hand to her, and she ran towards him.

"Daddy…!" She flung herself into his arms, holding him tightly. "Did you find Vicky?" she sobbed. "They burned the house."

"Vicky's fine, I got her out. She's with Auntie Adeline. Are you hurt?"

"No…"

The man looked at him. "Get in your car. Drive away. Don't look back."

"What about Amy?" Dane asked.

Amy shook her head, the gun now pointed at her head. "Please, just do what he asks."

A shot rang out and Amy's scream merged with the scream from the terrified child in his arms.

"That's a warning, you won't get another."

Dane pulled Jodie back towards the safety of the car. He didn't want her hurt.

"You can't leave Amy," Jodie protested. "They're

going to kill her."

"I'm not going to, but I need you safe."

A hand dropped on his shoulder and he jumped, turning.

"Nate, what took you so long?"

"Jodie, go with this officer," Nate said, his tone indicating she had no choice but to obey. "He'll sit with you in a marked patrol car. You'll be safe there. We'll get Amy back."

"OK, Uncle Nate. Take care, Dad." Jodie hugged Dane and did as she was told.

Dane looked from Nate to the DI. "I have to get Amy."

"The place is surrounded," DI Welsh said firmly. "They're not going anywhere. Let the armed response unit handle it."

Dane turned around. Amy was standing in the road by the war memorial, not moving. The car revved its engine over and over, bright lights illuminating her shaking figure. Then it reversed as far as it could go. The main beam came on and Amy raised a hand to shield her eyes. The engine revved again.

Shock hit Dane with full force. "He's going to run her over," he gasped.

The car started to move.

Dane launched himself into the road, running full pelt.

Amy just stood there.

"Amy!"

The car got closer.

Amy turned her head, her eyes widening as she saw Dane. "No, he'll hurt you, too."

Dane got nearer.

Amy shook her head.

Dane leapt into the air, grabbing Amy and pulling her with him out of the way of the car, just in time. Hot air blasted them as the car passed with millimeters to spare. He landed on top of her, shielding her with his body.

A police cruiser roared past in pursuit, blues and twos blaring. Other well hidden cars appeared almost from nowhere, and surrounded Saunders' car.

Dane looked down at Amy, pushing her hair out of the way. "Are you all right?"

"I think so. I'm sorry, I—"

"Later," Dane whispered. He leaned down, kissing her.

Running footsteps came over to them.

"Ewww," Jodie's voice filled his head, and he broke off.

"Ewww?" he asked, rolling off Amy and helping her to her feet. "Then don't look." He turned his back on her.

Amy didn't laugh as he expected, rather glanced at him in despair. "But you know the truth about me. How can you love me now? I'm a convicted criminal. You're a policeman."

Dane cradled her face gently, running the pad of his thumb along her bruised skin. He shivered as he stared into her eyes. How could he ever have doubted her? "Amy Childs, Amy Stabler, whatever your name is, you are still *my* Amy. And I still love you. Just promise me there are no more skeletons in your closet."

"And no more Mr. Scruffys in the kitchen. One of those is more than enough, thank you," Amy muttered.

"That thing is going in the rubbish as soon as I find it," Dane said firmly. "We can work everything else out, all of it. There is one condition though."

"What's that?"

He smiled. "You consider changing your name one last time."

Amy wound her fingers through his hair, lowering her tone to match his. "What do I change it to?"

Dane leaned in so only she could hear him. "Amy Philips," he whispered. He touched his lips to hers, kissing her with every ounce of passion his could find.

20

Amy sat on the gurney in the busy ED. "I'm fine."

"You've got a cracked head," Dane scolded. "And scratch marks on your cheek"

"And I'm fine."

"Don't argue, woman. If the doc says stay in overnight, then you stay in overnight."

"Where's Jodie?"

"In the next cubicle with Nate."

"Go be with her."

"She told me to come be here with you. But if you'd rather Nate hold your hand, then sure."

DI Welsh stuck her head around the curtain. "Amy, there's someone to see you. Dane, can we give them a moment?"

Dane nodded. "I'll be right outside."

Amy watched him go, holding her breath. Who could it be? Her heart leapt for joy as Ray came in, pushing a wheelchair. "Oh…"

Even though Dane had told her Rosalie wasn't dead, she hadn't dared believe. She thought perhaps he was just saying it to make her own death a little easier.

"Hello, Amy." Rosalie looked at her, straight-faced. "How are you?"

"Fine, though that isn't what the doctor says. What about you?" She pushed off the gurney, and closed her eyes, struggling to regain her balance.

"Been better."

Amy hugged her tightly, then when the hug wasn't reciprocated, let Ray help her back onto the gurney. "What happened?"

"Shouldn't that be my question?" Rosalie asked, her voice as hard as her eyes. "I mean my 'best friend,' or the person I thought was my best friend, let me think she was dead. Faked her own death, put me and my family in danger, because she couldn't trust me to keep a secret. Decided to run, after all we did for her, because she couldn't trust us. She took matters into her own hands instead of trusting God to work on the mess she made."

Amy's face burned and nausea rose in her throat. "It wasn't like that."

"No? Then tell me what it was like, because I don't understand! They kidnapped me. If those two men hadn't been there, they'd have taken Sara and killed her, too. They broke my arm, and…" Her voice trembled, and she broke off.

Ray put an arm around her. "Easy, love."

Rosalie shook her head. "She has to hear this. They tortured me wanting to know where you were. Then when I couldn't tell them, they showed me photos of you, alive and well, having a whale of a time… in the park and shopping and walking with the kids. Then they took me to the cliff and pushed me off. I thought I was going to die."

"But you didn't…" Amy whispered.

"No. The doctors don't think I'll walk again. I just hope God has something good to come out of this, because right now I can't see any.."

"I'm sorry." But deep down, Amy knew sorry wasn't ever going to be good enough for what she'd done.

Rosalie looked down at her hands. "So why did you leave?"

"He...he wanted me dead," Amy said. "I thought if I left, if I pretended to give him what he wanted..." Tears poured down her face. "It broke my heart leaving you and Ray, but I had no choice. I didn't want him to hurt you or Sara or...but he did and I'm so sorry..."

She turned away, sobbing. She'd ruined everything. She'd lost her best friend, gotten her back, only to lose her because of something she'd done.

The curtain swished, and Dane's arm and scent enveloped her. His voice spoke over her head. "DS Dane Philips, we spoke on the phone, Pastor."

Rosalie's voice trembled. "It's you. The man who saved Sara."

Dane spoke. "I'm sorry we couldn't stop them from taking you."

"He shot you."

"It's healing, but a small price to pay."

"The other man with you?"

"My partner. He's just behind that curtain, making sure my daughter doesn't do a runner."

"I'm not the one afraid of needles, Dad." Jodie's voice was indignant.

Amy looked up slowly to see Ray shake Dane's hand.

"Thank you for what you did. You saved my daughter, tried to save Rosie."

"I wish I could have done more."

"You did more than I could."

Dane reached into his pocket. "I've been asked to give you this. It's the number of our church pastor."

Amy tuned the men out and looked at Rosalie. "I don't expect you to forgive me," she whispered. "I hurt you, lied to you, you're right to be angry...to hate me."

"I don't hate you," Rosalie said. "I'm hurt, I'm mad and I really didn't want to come down here and see you, but Ray insisted."

Amy glanced at Ray. "I'm sorry."

"I'm just as hurt," he said quietly. "It'll take us a while to come to terms with this, but..."

"But?" she whispered. Was that a sliver of hope?

"We're prepared to work on it, if you are."

"I promise," she whispered, tears falling again.

Dane helped her off the bed and she knelt in front of Rosalie's wheelchair. This time, when she hugged her, Rosalie hugged her back.

She was going to have to deal with the consequences of doing the wrong thing for the rest of her life, but maybe together they'd get through this.

❧❦

A week later

Amy scrubbed the walls in the kitchen, trying to get rid of the smoke damage. Beside her, Vicky and Jodie worked with her in matching jeans, shirts, with scarves tied over their hair. She glanced up at Dane as he came in. He'd been talking to the builder for the last hour and a half. "How's it going? Has Mr. Wallac left yet?"

"Yes, just. You'll be pleased to know that he can rebuild it. Better than it was before."

Amy laughed. "Oh, is it going to be better, stronger and faster?"

Dane grinned. "Hopefully soundproof if Jodie is planning more music homework in the study." He moved over to Amy and wrapped his arms around her. "How's it going in here?"

"Slowly. Though why I'm bothering to remove smoke grime when there will be brick dust everywhere as well for months, I have no idea. Or are we moving out? We can't stay with Nate and Adeline too long. They won't have the room."

"Elliott says he can work while we live here. He'll cover the area with blue plastic sheeting which should keep most of the brick dust out."

Jodie looked up. "Vianne's going to have a baby cousin," she said.

Amy smiled. "I know; that's going to be really exciting."

Vicky tilted her head. "Can I have one?"

"A baby cousin?" Dane asked. "Not really, sweetie, because I don't have any brothers or sisters. And that's where cousins come from."

Her face fell. "Oh."

Dane hugged Vicky as he gazed at Amy. "You never did answer my question."

She looked puzzled. "What question? You asked me so many over the past few days that I can't remember one in particular."

He rolled his eyes. "About changing your name."

"Oh, that one." She grinned. "As I recall, you didn't give me a chance to answer it, before first kissing me and then threatening to arrest me for breaking my sentencing conditions."

Jodie's face fell. "Forget I ever called you a girly swot. Really Amy, are you in trouble *again*?"

Amy shook her head. "No, sweetie. Your dad asked if I'd change my name to Amy Philips."

Jodie and Vicky looked at each other. "He wants to

marry you?"

"I do," Dane said. He put an arm around each of the girls. "If you two agree."

They both nodded and turned expectant faces to Amy. "Please, Amy."

Amy grinned. "I'd love to change my name."

The girls cheered as Dane's arms went around her, and his lips found hers. Somewhere in the distance, as she lost herself in the emotions Dane stirred in her, she heard Jodie and Vicky talking.

"This means we go one better than Vianne. We might get a brother."

"Sister," Vicky whispered.

"It might be twins," Jodie said. "One of each."

Dane laughed. "Give us a chance, kids. I haven't even booked the church yet." He ran his fingers down Amy's face. "It's funny how things turn out, isn't it?"

"Yeah, it's just like I told Jodie. We mess things up and God straightens them out. Not how we'd imagine, but a whole load better."